Cutthroat Mafia

Lock Down Publications and Ca$h
Presents

Cutthroat Mafia

A Novel by *Ghost*

Lock Down Publications
P.O. Box 870494
Mesquite, Tx 75187

Visit our website @
www.lockdownpublications.com

First Edition April 2020
Printed in the United States of America

Lock Down Publications
Like our page on Facebook: Lock Down Publications @
www.facebook.com/lockdownpublications.ldp
Cover design and layout by: **Dynasty Cover Me**
Book interior design by: **Shawn Walker**
Edited by: **Lashonda Johnson**

Stay Connected with Us!

Text **LOCKDOWN** to 22828 to stay up-to-date with new releases, sneak peaks, contests and more…

Thank you.

Submission Guideline.

Submit the first three chapters of your completed manuscript to ldpsubmissions@gmail.com, subject line: Your book's title. The manuscript must be in a .doc file and sent as an attachment. Document should be in Times New Roman, double spaced and in size 12 font. Also, provide your synopsis and full contact information. If sending multiple submissions, they must each be in a separate email.

Have a story but no way to send it electronically? You can still submit to LDP/Ca$h Presents. Send in the first three chapters, written or typed, of your completed manuscript to:

LDP: Submissions Dept
Po Box 870494
Mesquite, Tx 75187

DO NOT send original manuscript. Must be a duplicate.

Provide your synopsis and a cover letter containing your full contact information.

Thanks for considering LDP and Ca$h Presents.

Dedications:

First of all, this book is dedicated to my Baby Girl 3/10, the love of my life and purpose for everything I do. As long as I'm alive, you'll never want nor NEED for anything. We done went from flipping birds to flipping books. The best is yet to come.

To LDP'S CEO- Ca$h & COO- Shawn:

I would like to thank y'all for this opportunity. The wisdom, motivation, and encouragement that I've received from you two is greatly appreciated.

The grind is real. The loyalty in this family is real. I'm riding with LDP 'til the wheels fall off.

THE GAME IS OURS !

Chapter 1

Baltimore, Maryland

LaShawn sat at the dining room table with her head down, staring at the overdue notices of bill emails that appeared on her phone. She blew air out of her jaws and shook her head in defeat. It was mid-March and there was still light snow falling from the sky outside of her duplex. The harsh winds blew causing the house to rattle. The shadows of the barren tree branches danced upon the walls of her place. She looked over the phone lost, feeling sick on the stomach imagining herself, and her six-year-old daughter, Lashonda being evicted for the second time in three months.

"Damn, I don't feel like goin' through this again," she whispered. She placed the phone back on the table and rested her face in her hands.

Her brother, Preston came down the back steps from the attic, opening the door that led into the small kitchen. He stood five-feet-nine inches tall, stocky, with muscular arms and a small gut. He sported a low cut that he kept nappy on top and edged up all around. He slipped into the kitchen and retrieved the box of *Cookie Crisp* cereal from the top of the refrigerator. He side-stepped and opened the cupboard, taking a nice sized bowl out, setting it on the table along with the cereal. He glanced over at his sister, LaShawn with her head down.

He eased into the dining room and stood beside her placing, his hand on her shoulder. "Yo', sis, what's good wit' you?"

LaShawn simply handed him the phone. "I don't know what I'm finna do. Ain't no way I can come up with even half of this money. I wish the factory would've told us ahead of time that they were about to be laying people off. How the hell am I supposed to pay these bills, Preston?"

Preston scrolled through the emails, calculating their cost. The total came to forty-five hundred dollars. He swallowed his spit. Not only did he not have any idea where that kind of money was going to come from, but he was freshly released from prison after serving three years for robbery, and aggravated assault. He hadn't been home for more than two weeks, and he could already tell that the struggle was real.

“Damn, sis, what that nigga Pooh on? He ain't tryna help you figure this shit out?” He referred to Lashonda's baby’s father.

She shrugged. “Pooh is a deadbeat and you know it. He don’t care about nobody, but himself. He’s always been that way, and I don't think he will ever change. Besides, I don't need him or no other nigga. I got this, I'll figure this shit out, I always do.” She grabbed her phone back and lifted her forearm from the thirty-day eviction notice she'd received earlier that morning from her landlord.

Preston sat in the chair across from her, lost in thought. Though he’d only been out for a few weeks, he wasn't about to allow LaShawn and his niece to be evicted, or without their simple necessities. That wasn't in his DNA to sit back and not make it happen. He looked across the table into LaShawn’s brown eyes, and saw worry painted across her pretty caramel face. That made him even sicker. LaShawn had been the only one who stood by him while he was on lock, and he felt like it was his duty now that he was home, to make sure that she nor his niece didn't need for anything.

He hopped up. “That's forty-five hundred on those bills. How much you paying for rent?”

LaShawn sighed. “Boy, you just got home, don't even worry about it.” She stood up, depression set in. She wondered how her life had gotten to such a sunken place. She felt both stressed and mentally depleted.

"I don't care about that. I asked you how much is rent?"

"Nine-hundred, for an overall total of fifty-four-hundred dollars. Where in the hell am I gon' get that kind of money?"

Preston stepped around the table and pulled her into his embrace. "Yo,' I got this, Goddess. You already know I'd never let you do this shit on your own." He kissed her forehead and held her tighter.

"But I don't want you doin' nothin' stupid, Preston. Things will get better. We just might have to struggle for a little while. I mean it ain't like we aren't used to it anyway. We've struggled our whole lives."

Preston nodded. His brain started trying to find a solution for their many financial problems. He wasn't trying to see prison again. He'd lost twenty pounds over those last few years that he'd been inside and had never felt sicklier. He also hated being around so many nasty dudes at one time. But he was the only man left breathing that LaShawn could fully depend on, and that meant he had to step his game up and jump back into the same streets that sought to kill him before he was incarcerated.

Baltimore was merciless and packed with cold-hearted savages. It was a hard knock life of a city, but Preston was born and raised in the gutters of Baltimore, and its numerous struggles. In his mind, he was prepared to do whatever it took to provide for his family, and he didn't care about the risks or the other sharks in the water because he was one as well.

He took a step back and kept his big hands on LaShawn's shoulders. "Look, sis, I promise you on my soul that before the end of this week. I'll have every red cent that you need. I don't want you worrying about this shit no more because I got you. You hear me?" He stared directly into her eyes.

LaShawn nodded. “I hear you, Preston, but I don't want you gettin’ into any trouble for me. At the very least, go out and get a job, and we can go from there. I mean it might not cover all the bills, but at least, I will know those people can't lock you back up. When are you scheduled to see your probation officer?”

“In a week, I'll have that money before then. I ain't tryna hear none of that shit you talkin’ about. I'm about to hit up this jungle. That’s that.”

***

An hour later, Macho pulled his red Jeep Wrangler in front of LaShawn's duplex. He beeped the horn three times, adjusting the Tech .9 on his lap. There was a red bandana around the handle of the automatic weapon, and he had it souped up with a bump stock and a hundred round clip.

Macho and Preston had served their final two years in prison together, and while serving their bids the pair had grown real close. Macho was five-feet-eleven inches tall, slender with long dreads and skin as dark as night. Macho didn't like nobody, but for some reason, after he'd watched Preston beat a two-hundred-fifty pounds dude in prison half to death, he'd taken a liking to him. When the big gorilla's homie tried to jump in to help him fight, Preston. Macho gave him a three-piece combination that knocked him out cold. Ever since that day, Macho watched Preston's back and Preston watched his.

Preston came out of the house and slid into the passenger's seat of the Jeep. He shook up with Macho. “What's to it, kid?”

Macho reached under the seat and handed Preston a .9 millimeter. “Yo,’ it ain't nothin’, Boss. But here put this bitch on yo’ lap just in case one of these goofies try a nigga while we rollin'. I got a play for a few gees, too. I know you need to hear that."

Preston was already geeked up, he took the .9mm and cocked it. His eyes scanned LaShawn's block for any potential threats, he saw none other than the few Jack Boys who hung out at the end of the block. He wasn't worried about them, though. They hunted Dope Boys, so as far as they knew, he was broke. Macho rolled in a Jeep Wrangler, so he had broke written all over him, too.

"What's the play, Son?" Preston asked.

Macho dug into the console grabbing two Pink Mollies out of it, popping both in his mouth. He grabbed two more and handed them to Preston. "Yo, my brother, George, been working for this Arab ma'fucka at his bodega. He's the meat man. Anyway, George was tellin' me that every Tuesday his boss takes all the money from the safe that he'd made the whole week and take it to the bank. He doesn't do this until the store closes at ten o'clock at night. It's eight o'clock, right now. I wanna hit his ass up tonight to see what we get." Macho slid his hand around the handle of his Tech as he rolled past the Jack Boys on the corner. He mugged them, making sure they saw the red rag around his neck. He was praying one of them did something stupid or out of line.

"That's what you came up with? You're trying to rob some punk-ass store. Really?" Preston didn't know about that. He knew George was a hype. Dope addicts were always for sale. Not only could the hood use them to get information, but so did the police. Preston imagined laying in a prison cell all over again, sadness immediately overtaking him.

"Hell yeah, because it's sweet. All we gon' do is go in there at about nine fifty-five and lay that bitch down. My brother will already be inside and gon' assist us with what we have to do. He knows where the Arab dude keeps his safe, and he done fucked up and gave him the combination. Shit super sweet. All we gotta do is make it happen."

Preston wasn't completely sold on the endeavor. He still didn't trust George. "Yo', kid, what is George hoping to come away with? I know he ain't doin' this shit just for the fun of it. What's his agenda?"

"Bruh, say just hit him with a few hunnit. We do that and we good." Macho kept rolling before he looked over at Preston and saw his head lowered, holding his chin. Preston was in deep thought, and this irritated Macho because he was sure that Preston was second-guessing the mission. "Fuck you got to lose, nigga? You already said you need to get your hands on some cream so you can handle shit at home. Well, this is the first lick, and we gotta hit this bitch to get started. Ma'fuckas need some money in their pocket, right now."

Preston remembered the saddened look on LaShawn's face before he'd left the house. It had broken his cold heart. He didn't like seeing his sister struggling. He didn't like imagining his niece out in the cold or forced to sleep on some random family member's couch. Nobody could be trusted, and he refused to allow them to hit rock bottom like that. While he didn't trust George, if it came down to it, he knew he wouldn't hesitate to knock his brains out of his skull, even if he had to do it behind Macho's back.

"Say, Dunn, it's good. Set that shit up. Tell that nigga George we about to come through that bitch and cause hell in a few. I'm wit' it, but I'm lettin' you know right now, I ain't goin' back to prison, B, word up. If shit starts lookin' fishy, I'ma wet somethin' and leave the Coroner to dry it off."

"Fuck you think I'ma do?" Macho scoffed. "Being around all those nasty, dirtbag, ass niggas in the joint was enough to wake me all the way up. 'Yo, fuck seein' the inside of a cell again, B. Word up, I'm holdin' court in the streets from here on out. Only time handcuffs coming across these wrists again is when I'm getting freaky wit' a bitch." He snickered.

"I ain't even fuckin' wit' it den. I have that metal shit, B. Yo', I'm fuckin' wit' you the long way tho'. We gon' handle dis bidness, and den we gon' get to it from there. I gotta make shit happen for my family. If not me, then who?"

Preston imagined how it felt holding Lashonda in his arms when she was born. He couldn't believe that Pooh would allow her to suffer along with LaShawn the way that he was, especially since he was out here supposedly checking a big bag. It made no sense to him. He decided right then that Pooh would be added to the list of Dope boys that he would place on his plate to nourish his pockets.

'*I'ma crush his bitch ass soon enough,*' he thought, laughing.

Macho gave him the side-eye. "Yo, I can tell you're over there on some sadistic shit. Whatever you wit, you already know I am, too. We are in this shit together. Word up." He held out his hand.

Preston shook up with him. "You already know that. Let's handle this bidness."

Chapter 2

It was nine-fifty at night. A white ski-masked Preston scooted backward until his back was on the brick wall that made up some of the Arab's Bodega that he and Macho were set to run in. He peeked from the side of the store's gangway, surveying the block. All was quiet and desolate. The Bodega was located on the corner of the street directly in front of the metro bus stop. This worried Preston, he couldn't afford for him or Macho to be seen by a city bus driver. The driver could easily call the police, and because the driver would be dispatching the authorities, Preston figured they would get there much faster.

Macho slid next to him with a .40 Glock in his left hand, and his face covered with a white ski mask as well. He scanned the atmosphere and grew anxious. “I'm ready to get my hands on some bread, bruh. This broke shit is for dem other niggas.” He cocked the Glock, easing closer to the exit of the gangway. “You ready?”

Though Preston felt bouts of apprehension, he knew it was now or never. He nodded, frowning under his mask. “Let's get it, Slime.”

Macho glanced at his cheap plastic, clear jail watch and saw that it was nine fifty-five on the dot. He squatted, then he walked around to the front of the store. He pulled open the door as the bells chimed indicating that a customer was entering. It smelled like spice ham and cheap incense. Arab music played out the speakers that were hanging in the four corners of the store. There was a heavy-set, Puerto Rican male heading out of the Bodega with a gallon of milk, and five dollars' worth of Hog Head cheese.

Pow! Macho stepped right up to him and knocked him out with one punch.

The Puerto Rican man flew into the chip rack sending Potato Chips flying all over the front of the store. Preston rushed past Macho and hopped over the counter of the Bodega before the Arab could reach for his trusted shotgun that he kept under the counter. Preston had the barrel of his gun thrust in his Adam's apple, slamming him into the bottles of alcohol that were directly behind the cashier. They fell all over them and crashed to the floor exploding.

"Bitch ass nigga, we don't wanna murder you, but I don't give a fuck about doin' it either. Take me to the ma'fuckin' safe, or you gon' feel this hot copper in yo' ass."

Macho locked the front door to the store before running to the back. When he got to the meat counter, he spotted George bent down beside the metal sink that he used to wash his filthy hands. Macho aimed his gun at him. "Get yo' punk ass over here, right now!"

George was five-feet-nine inches tall with a slim frame. His face was full of craters from heavy usage of Methamphetamine. He was without an upper row of teeth, so his mouth formed a sideways *M* whenever he pressed his lips together.

"Don't kill me. Please don't kill me!" he hollered, playing along. He couldn't believe his little brother was actually hitting the store. He could already imagine the dope he would be cooking before the night was out.

Macho wasn't with that acting nonsense. He was dead set on treating George just like he would any other victim. He hopped the meat counter and grabbed George by the throat. He picked him up in the air with one hand and slammed him to the ground as hard as he could, knocking the wind out of him.

"Stay yo' pussy ass, right there. You get up, I'm smoking you," he meant it, too.

The last thing he needed was for George to screw up, and either call him by his name or just to do something stupid that they couldn't come back from. His best bet was to leave the man on the ground where he was. Macho bent down and rocked him with a left hook, knocking George out.

Preston slung the Arab over the desk inside the man's office. He knocked the laptop onto the floor, along with his cellphone. Preston grabbed him and threw him in front of the steel safe. He pressed the .9mm to his head. "Open that bitch, Kid! Hurry the fuck up, time is money."

The Arab felt blood ooze out of his nose. His jaw felt broken. One of his ribs was popped out of place. He had never been in so much pain. He began to say a silent prayer to give him strength. He felt Preston grabbed the back of his head. The next thing he knew, his face was crashing into the safe. "Okay! Okay! Please, I give you the money. I give it to you!"

"You, betta hurry the fuck up!" Preston warned, his heart pounding within his chest.

"Okay." The Arab opened the panel of the Secure Tek safe. He placed his hand on the digital screen, punched in the code, and waited until the safe buzzed and popped open.

As soon as Preston saw it open, he slung the handle of his .9 mm into the back of the Arab's head dropping him to the floor, knocking him out cold. Preston stepped over him and grabbed the empty garbage can. He took the bag out of it and opened the safe all the way. There inside, he counted about twelve thousand dollars in cash. He searched deeper into it, finding the rest of it empty. He threw the bag down and ran out of the office.

Macho had a big black garbage bag full of alcohol and cigarettes. When Preston ran into the front of the store, he dropped it and aimed his gun at him. He breathed a sigh of relief when he realized who it was. "Fuck bruh, I almost smoked yo' ass."

Preston waved him off. "Let's get the fuck up out of here before Twelve come. Come on."

George came down the aisle of laundry products holding his jaw. "Why the fuck you hit me so hard, Macho?" He spit blood on the floor and continued to come their way.

Macho clenched his teeth. "Nigga shut the fuck up!"

"You hit me too hard. My jaw feels broken." He staggered and held himself by a shelf full of Tide detergent.

"Yo', I'ma smoke this old nigga if he don't shut the fuck up, Blood. Word up." Preston felt himself getting hyped up. He didn't like George or no other male for that matter outside of Macho.

Macho stepped into George's face. "Nigga, lay yo' ass down and see this shit through. I'ma straighten you when you get home tonight. Now do it, fuck nigga." He grabbed George by the neck and slung him into the rack of Bounce sheets before he took off running out of the store.

Preston stood there with his finger on the trigger. He wanted to stank George. That's what his first mind told him. He couldn't trust him. He mugged him and watched George struggle to his feet. Preston shook his head. "Nall fuck that, I ain't goin' back to prison." He aimed his gun.

"Come on, nigga! Let's get the fuck out of here!" Macho yelled from the doorway, snapping Preston out of his zone. Seconds later, the pair was jumping into their stolen car, speeding down the alley twelve thousand dollars richer.

***

LaShawn sat on the couch across from Pooh and watched the light-skinned, hazel-eyed, six-feet tall, pretty boy interact with their daughter who was a spitting image of him. Pooh had his long dreadlocks pulled in a thick money green rubber band that matched the attire he wore. LaShawn sat there scorned. She hated him, while the softer part of her loved his trifling ass at the same time.

She stood up and rubbed her palms on the thighs of her Walmart jeans. “Okay, Pooh, time is up. It’s time for you to go. I need to get her ready for school tomorrow, and myself ready for work.”

Pooh ignored her and continued to hug on six-year-old, Lashonda. He kissed her forehead. “Baby, daddy gotta go, but I want you to know that I love you. Here.” He gave her a blue-faced hundred- dollar bill.

Lashonda took it and smiled. “Thank you, daddy. Next time you come can I go with you?” He glanced over at LaShawn. “Yo’, we gon’ have to see what yo’ mama say. You know she be trippin’ and shit.”

“Uh-uh, don't do that, Pooh. Don't curse around her and try to turn my daughter against me. That ain't cool.” She reached out for Lashonda's hand. “Let's go lil’ girl. Say good night and go turn on the water for your bath.”

“Yes, ma'am.” She hugged Pooh again. “Goodnight, daddy. I love you.” She broke into a fit of tears as she stomped down the hallway.

“Alright now, don't make me pop them lil’ legs girl!” LaShawn chastised. She knew it was going to be a rough night.

Every time Lashonda spent time with Pooh, it made parenting her daughter more difficult afterward. Pooh had a habit of saying all the right things that would get Lashonda on his side, but he never had any intentions of following through with anything he said. That irked LaShawn to an unexplainable point.

"Yes, ma'am," Lashonda whimpered, before going into the bathroom.

"Don't be makin' it seem like you gon' put yo' hands on my baby 'cuz she wanna see her daddy. Don't have me set this mafucka up. You already know how I get down." He adjusted the Patek watch on his left wrist that was draped in crush diamonds.

LaShawn rolled her eyes. "Nigga, whatever. Since you're here, right now acting all high and mighty, givin' out hundreds and shit. Why don't you help me with some of these bills?"

Pooh laughed. "When was the last time I hit that pussy?"

LaShawn jerked her head back. "Boy, please, your reputation is horrible. You fuckin' every bitch and they mama in Baltimore. If I want to catch something, I'll go kiss somebody with the Coronavirus." She rolled her eyes and got ready to walk past him to the front door.

Pooh pulled her aggressively to his body. He backed up and slammed her against the wall, pinning her there with his massive frame. She struggled against him. He looked into her eyes. "Who the fuck you think you playin' wit', huh? Don't you know that you gon' always be, my bitch? I don't give a fuck who you think I'm fuckin'."

"Get off me, Pooh. Ain't nobody got time for this bullshit. If you can't help me with these bills, then you ain't got shit to say to me or my daughter. That's how that's gon' go."

Pooh trailed his hands down her back and cuffed her soft ass cheeks, squeezing them and sucking on her neck. "I ain't got no problem helpin' you with yo' bills, Shorty. You got my daughter. Why wouldn't I help you?" He slowly eased her skirt upward until her bottom cheeks were exposed. He licked her neck, before biting into it.

LaShawn felt shivers vibrate through her body. Her nipples became erect and her pussy moistened. She hated his effect on her. He'd had it ever since they were fifteen and she'd given him her virginity. "Well, my bills come up to a little more than five thousand dollars. How much you gon' help me out with?"

Pooh sucked on her neck and slipped his fingers under her ass cheeks. His fingers crept into her thong from the back. He played over her warm pussy lips. His middle finger searched for her opening. "That depends, you gon' bless me with some of this gushy?" His middle finger found its mark and slipped deep into her.

LaShawn closed her eyes and moaned deep within her throat. She couldn't control it as much as she wanted to. "Why I always gotta do somethin' first? How about you hit my hand and I'll do what I gotta do for you?" She reached between them and took a hold of his hard dick, squeezing it inside of her small hand.

Pooh closed his eyes as he humped into her hand. He stopped and turned her around, with one grasp, he thrust her into the air, making her wrap her thighs around him. He unzipped his pants, exposing himself. He found her opening and slid in with one motion.

"Fuck!" The first thing that came across LaShawn's mind was that it was too late. He was already ten inches deep in her pussy. She prayed that he was clean and would keep his word. She held his shoulders and threw her head back. "I hate you, Pooh! Uh! Uh! I swear I hate you!" she screamed.

Pooh threw her up and down over and over. Her pussy gripped his dick, milking him. His knees grew weak. He lowered her to the floor, watching his dick go in and out of her as her pussy opened and closed around his dick, wetting it up. He sucked her neck, fucking her as hard as he could. He didn't know the next time he'd be able to get the pussy again because paying even one of her bills was out of the question. He rolled his back and growled, his nut building up. He forced her knees to her chest, cumming deep within her.

LaShawn hated herself for being so weak, so vulnerable. She couldn't believe she had succumbed to his game once again. She pushed Pooh off her. “Get off of me.”

Pooh stood up and continued to buss his nut all over LaShawn with a smile on his face. “Fuck you then. That's why I ain't givin’ yo’ ratchet ass shit.” He finished his business and left her on the floor crying.

***

That night Preston eased into LaShawn's bedroom and located her purse. His take home from the twelve-thousand-dollar lick was five thousand even. He took all of it and stuffed it into her purse. He crept to her bed and planted a kiss on her cheek. “I told you I had you, I ain't done either.” He pulled the sheet over her frame and left her room.

LaShawn hoped out of the bed, grabbed the money out of her purse, and counted it faster than a bank teller. When she came to five thousand dollars, she fell to her knees in tears. “Thank you, Jesus.”

Though she was grateful to have had the money she needed, she couldn’t help but worry about where Preston had gotten the money. She slid back into bed, slowly drifting off to sleep, plotting her revenge against Pooh.

Chapter 3

Chick! Chick! Macho cocked the sawed-off, five-shot automatic shotgun and held it out at his reflection in the mirror. "Nigga, if I was anybody other than myself, I would body me before we even get started on this Jack Boy shit. I been a hustler my whole life, that shit takes too long. This layin' niggas down shit is quick and urgent. I call it priority money."

Preston was lost in thought as he sat on Macho's basement couch. "Yo', I think that nigga, Pooh, was at my sister's crib last night."

"And, so what if he was?" Macho went back to imagining himself blowing a nigga's head off. He smiled at the mental imagery. "What's yo' beef with Blood ass?"

"Other than him being a deadbeat? I ain't never liked, Kid. I had to fuck him up a few times growing up. I hate that my sister even got involved with his bum ass." He took his double cup and sipped from his Lean, it burned his throat.

"That nigga ain't no bum. He be havin' some major paper now that his brother, Burleigh, home. You know that fool fuck with them Colombians and they be hitting him hard. Word on the street is that Pooh is the brickman now. I thought you knew that?" Macho lowered his gun and sat on the couch. He picked up a half of blunt out of the ashtray and sparked it dismissing his probation officer's orders to not partake with the drug.

Preston felt like he'd been slapped in the face. "You mean to tell me, this nigga out here having major money like that and he can't help my sister take care of, Lashonda? What type of shit is that?" He felt himself becoming vexed. He imagined Pooh's face and started to shake. He'd never liked him and hated him even more after LaShawn had Lashonda. Preston disliked deadbeat fathers and swore that whenever he had a child he would never be one of them.

"Bruh, this is Baltimore. Most of the niggas running around this bitch don't take care of their kids. And most of the hoes got a child by each nigga in the click. You know how this shit go. You just taking that shit personal because it's your sister that's rocking with a deadbeat. I feel that, and I'm 'bout whatever you 'bout."

Preston stood up. "You say he the brickman now for real?" Preston lowered his eyes. His mind was racing a hundred miles an hour.

"That's what the word is all through Guilford." Guildford was the neighborhood both Preston and Macho was from. Guilford was the slums of Baltimore.

"Well, if he don't start looking out for my sister and my niece soon, I'ma have to take a good look at this nigga and see what kind of chips he got stashed away. If a ma'fucka don't wanna take care of his responsibilities, then we got ways to make that shit happen on our own. Yo', word is bond, I'm so close to turning up. If that animal shit come out of me, Kid, it's gon' be one. That's my word."

Macho smiled and aimed his shotgun at the wall. "I'll be glad when it do come out of you so we can hit the ground running life savages. I don't know how long I can be with this passive shit. I wanna start eating these niggas for breakfast."

George came partway down the stairs and stuck his head out far enough for them to see him. He cursed under his breath and came the rest of the way down the stairs. He held the hand of a white, skinny Meth addict female. He was high as a kite, and she was looking to get high on his dime. "Say, Macho, I need the basement for a minute."

"I don't give no fuck what you need. Y'all better take y'all hype asses upstairs to the attic. Me and the homie chilling down here discussing business, beat it."

George was defiant, he waved Preston off. “Man, lil’ dude ain't on shit. Y'all can talk that bullshit somewhere else. I'm trying to kick it with my 'ol lady.” He looked the female up and down. Her hair was stringy, and she was without teeth. She was skinny, her skin was yellowish. She was just as sick as she looked.

“Man, fuck you and this Bitch. Y'all take y'all nasty asses upstairs to the attic and do what you do. Ain't shit happening down here. Word up.” Macho grabbed a rag and began to wipe down the shotgun.

George felt like he was being punked by his little brother. He didn't like Macho flexing on him in front of his new woman. He felt like he needed to stand up for himself. He side-eyed, Preston. “Fuck is you looking at, nigga? This ain't got shit to do with you.”

Preston looked from his left to his right. He was sure George wasn't talking to him, but once he confirmed that he was. He pushed his white girl out of the way and stepped into his face. “Fuck on yo’, bird boy?” Preston clenched his jaw muscles, riled up. He was already vexed off Pooh's news, he needed an outlet for his anger.

George looked into his eyes and swallowed his spit. He was nervous. He wasn't expecting that response from Preston. His girlfriend looked up at him to see what he was about to do. She was already nervous because Macho held the shotgun in his hands, but her need for the Methamphetamine was too great. She was willing to be in the most dangerous of situations in order to get some for free, especially because she was broke.

“Nigga, I'm telling you, right now. If Preston gets to whooping yo’ ass I ain't helping you. You think you too tough,” Macho said this without even looking up at him while continuing to polish his gun.

George smacked his lips. “Preston, ain't gon’ do shit to me. I don't know why y'all think it’s sweet and get up out of my face, Preston!” He pushed him as hard as he could.

Preston flew backward but not before he could hit George with a right hook. Preston fell on the couch and hopped up with animal quickness. George twisted and fell to one knee. Preston rushed him pushing George's woman out of the way. George stood up, Preston picked him up into the air and slammed him down with brute strength. George's back popped, the back of his head hit the ground. He grew dizzy.

Preston stood over him breathing hard. “Nigga, you, betta quit playing with me. I ain't the one.” He stepped away from him and shook up with Macho. “I'ma fuck with you later. I gotta be up out of here.”

“Know that, Fammo. I'ma hit yo’ phone in a few hours. I'ma see if anything else shaking and let you know what's good.”

“That works.” He mugged George on his way out of the door.

George stood up and nodded his head with bitter revenge on his mind. “Yeah, you got me lil’ nigga. It’s all good.” He was jaded, he laughed to himself. “It’s all good.”

***

That night Preston sat across from his mother, Ilene while she sat on the sofa and got ready to shoot her dope. The sight always angered and humbled him. Even though Ilene was strung out on Heroin she was still his heart. She rubbed the alcohol pad over the faint vein located on her inner thigh, there was already a belt wrapped around it. She took the ready-made syringe and stuck the needle into her thigh, before injecting herself with the poor-quality dope. She closed her eyes and licked her lips.

Preston lowered his head. "Mama, you know I always hate when you gotta do this crap. When are you going to let me put you in rehab?" He felt his eyes getting glossy. Ilene was the one person who he sought to derive his strength from. When he saw her weak it hurt him.

"Baby, ain't no rehab can cure me of the sickness that I have. It's all up here." She pointed to her temple. Ilene was five-feet-two inches tall, dark-skinned, with a bald head, and very skinny. Her sunken eyes were brown.

"When was the last time that you ate anything?" He stood up and walked into her kitchen. Two big rats ran past his foot screeching loudly. Ilene's cat was on the chase. Preston was used to the living conditions. He didn't even flinch. Her kitchen floor was littered with roaches of all sizes. They were so brazened they didn't even run when he stepped close to them. He got to the refrigerator and pulled it open. He was met with a putrid smell. He pinched his nose and frowned. The inside of Ilene's refrigerator was empty with the exception of a spoiled jar of mayonnaise that had turned blue. He found that troubling.

"Mama, you ain't even got no food in here." He closed the refrigerator door and cursed under his breath. "Man, when was the last time that you ate? You still ain't answer that question."

Ilene staggered into the kitchen scratching her head. "Boy, I don't know. Why are you asking me all these questions anyway? You think you, my daddy?" She smiled at him showcasing her toothless mouth.

"No, ma'am. But I am your only son, so it is my job to make sure you are well taken care of. Despite what's taking place here, I love you." He walked over to her and kissed her forehead.

She wrapped her arms around his waist and rested her face on his chest. “You're going to be somethin’ great one of these days, baby. Mama just hopes that she is around to see it. You're bigger than Guilford, Preston. You are going to be somebody that everybody knows. You mark those words. I believe in you.”

“Thank you, mama, but I wish you believed in yourself more than you do me. I need you to be around for a long time. Why don't you let me get you some help? Please, my Queen.” He rested his lips on her sweaty forehead.

She hugged him tighter. “You can't help me, baby.” Her eyes became low, she nodded for a second. When she came back to her knees were getting weak and she fell against him.

Preston picked her up and carried her to her bedroom. He laid her down on the bed and pulled her shoes off. He made sure her head was resting on her pillow. He rubbed her forehead. “I know that you are stronger than this beautiful. You are my mother. You are the most important person in this world to me. There is no amount of success that I could ever reach that would make me feel any way if you aren't healthy and by my side. I need you, my Queen, and your son isn't afraid to admit this.”

Ilene closed her eyes and shook her head in dismay. “I don't understand why you love me so much, Preston. Damn boy! Don't you know that I hate myself? All I want to do is to get high and be left alone by that world out there. I wanna live my days in peace and harmony. When the good Lord comes to get me, I will be ready. I just hope that I am high one last time here on earth.” She closed her eyes back. “I would love to see you bless me with a grandbaby, though. That would be amazing.”

“I'm not ready to have a child yet, mama. Before I even think about popping off one of these sistahs, I have to be sure

I can invest my best eighteen years and nine months to both the mother and the child. deadbeat niggas make me wanna murder they—" He caught himself. He took a deep breath and blew it out.

The cat came into the room with a rat in its mouth. The rat was dripping blood. The cat put the rat on the floor and got ready to lick its paws when the rat flipped over and took off running right into the wall at full speed breaking its on neck. The cat dabbed at it with its paw. Once it, saw, it was unmoving it walked out of the room bored.

"Baby, you feel how you feel about deadbeats because your father was one. You just remember how he left us to fend for ourselves. That man didn't care about nobody but himself. I've been wronged a lot in my life by many different people. But I only hate one person, and that person is yo' punk ass daddy." She patted the bed next to her.

Preston climbed on it and laid next to Ilene. He held her and kissed her cheek. "It's all good mama because I promise you, I'ma pull us out of this struggle. I don't know how, and I don't know when. But I promise you on my soul that we will not be lost within this struggle for too much longer. We will be living like Kings and Queens soon. Trust your, baby."

"I do, I know that you are meant to be a king. You are not like these other men. You have deep-seated greatness inside of you, and I can't wait until it comes out. I love you son. Please never forget that." She hugged him and began to nod.

Preston laid there determined to make it out of the Baltimore trenches with his family. He was tired of struggling. Tired of being a have not. He needed to make it happen for his family's sake and he vowed to meet death before he didn't come through for his beloveds.

Chapter 4

"Man, explain this shit to me one more time because you making it seem like it's too easy. I know damn well, it can't be." Preston poured the Hennessy in his glass and filled it halfway. He sat on the couch and took two strong swallows from it. He wanted to smoke some bud real bad, but he was scheduled to see his probation officer in a few hours. The Hennessy was a risk within itself.

"Look, Preston, damn. This shit is super simple. I fuck with this Puerto Rican nigga name, Marco. He runs packs for the Ricans over there on Wilson Street. He do drop-offs and pickups for them eight hours out of the day, sometimes twelve. Long story short, once again, I know this nigga's routine, and I know how he gets down. I been watching him real closely. I'm telling you, we can hit both the trap he's running packs back and forth to, and we can hit him on his way back from getting paid after making whatever drop off he would have just done.

"The best day to knock him off is on a Sunday. He done jacked, running his mouth way too much and told me that's when he makes the most money, and their trap is loaded to the fullest. I wanna hit his nigga, the only thing about it is if we do, we might have to kill everybody up in there." Macho shrugged his shoulders. "But you know I don't give a fuck, though."

Preston sat and played with the hairs on his chin. He thought about Ilene, and the condition he'd left her in. He wanted to get her help so bad. He also wanted to move both LaShawn and Lashonda out of the slums of Guildford. He worried about them and their safety every second that he was out of their presence. In a way, he felt forced to follow behind Macho and his lick pickings. "Look, man, I'm down, but I wanna be in the presence of Marco before we hit his ass. I need to see what kind of nigga he is. I wanna gauge his character. I ain't never been around a Puerto Rican like that, but I heard that the ones over there on Wilson Street are lunatics and they don't play about their bread. So, I need to see what's good."

"That's cool with me. He throwing a lil' get together tonight for his sister Kayley's twentieth birthday. He invited me, and I'm inviting you. We can roll out there and see what it do. That way you can spend some time in his presence, and I can pick his brain some more. Also, it's gon' be plenty of bad bitches there. I wanna fuck wit' a few of them." He jumped up and dusted off his clothes. "How much of that bread you got left? I need a few hunnit."

"You popped, I ain't got a pot to piss in, right now. So, I don't know what to tell you." Preston stood up as well. "I'm finna get back to the crib and get dressed as best as I can. I'll see you tonight."

"Yep." Macho reached under the couch and grabbed his .40 Glock.

He needed some pocket change and he knew just how to get it. There was no way, he was about to go to anybody's party broke and busted. Especially when it was about to be flooded with women.

***

It was a dark and windy night when Macho pulled up in front of Marco's two-story house five hours later with Preston sitting in the passenger's seat. Instead of hitting one lick, Macho had caught two dope boys slipping and had come up on three thousand dollars, and two ounces of Kush. He spent a thousand on an outfit and gave Preston a thousand. That left him with one. He felt secure having a little bread in his pocket. He looked up at the house where Marco stayed and saw the strobe lights going off on the inside through the window. The block was packed with cars. The music was loud enough to be heard from where they sat.

Preston ran his hand over his waves, rubbing the grease into hair pattern as much as he could. “Let's go, bruh. What you gotta text him or somethin’?”

Macho was already finishing up the text to let Marco know that he was there. “Yeah, hopefully, he comes on to the doe. These Ricans be acting real funny around this ma’fucka. I ain't tryna have no discrepancies.” He grabbed his .40 and tucked it into his waistband.

Preston did the same with his .9 mm. He had never been on Wilson Street before because he knew the Spanish dudes ran it with an iron fist. It was rumored that a lot of them were racist and didn't mess with the Blacks. Preston didn't know how true that was, but he wasn't taking no chances.

“Bruh, make sure you watch my back, you already know I got yours. Don't take yo’ happy ass in here and get lost. Remember we are on a mission. Today is Friday, if we trying to hit this lick by Sunday then all of our ducks have to be in a row.”

“I hate when you talk to me like I don't know what's really good. I got this, Bruh. Money is the motive.” He nodded his head. “Look, there go Marco fat ass, right there.”

Marco shielded his eyes and looked off the porch. He spotted Macho's Jeep Wrangler and snickered. He threw his arms up. “Hey, Chico! Let's roll.”

“Where you say you know this fool from again?” Preston adjusted his gun again. He scanned the neighborhood and didn't find any reason to believe that they were in danger although his survival senses were heightened.

"We used to steal cars together back in the day, it's a long story. I'll tell you later. For now, let's handle this bidness." He opened the door to the Jeep and threw his arms up. "Marco, what's up, Papi?"

Marco stepped off the porch and shook up with him. "Nothing, Chico, y'all are missing the party. We better get inside. Who is he?" Marco nodded his head toward Preston. He was five-feet-six inches tall, brown-skinned, and heavy set. He had naturally curly hair and a big mole on the right side of his face.

"This is my right-hand, Preston. He's like my brother. Preston this is Marco."

Macho stepped out of the way so both men could shakeup. He knew Preston didn't like dudes and he was hoping that he'd at least play along so they could get closer to Marco.

Preston balled his hand into a fist and bumped his against Marco's. "What's good, Boss?"

"It's all good. Hey, long as you're cool with Macho you're cool with me vamanos." He motioned for them to follow him.

***

Preston nodded his head at the Reggaeton music coming out of the speakers. He didn't know what they were saying, but the beat was causing his head to bob. The party was packed with thirty people. There were two large speakers supplying the guests with music, and a vibration that made the bottoms of their feet itch. The strobe lights flashed on and off and made them feel as if they were walking and operating in slow motion. The house smelled like weed and cigarette smoke. People were popping every kind of pill they could get their hands on, and just as many brands of liquor.

Preston posted up by the hallway next to the living room with a pair of dark shades over his eyes. He wanted to see and remember as many faces as he could, especially the males. He knew that after they hit Marco there was a major chance the majority of the Latin dudes he saw at this party were going to be at their heads if Marco was ever able to finger them as being the ones that screwed him and his guys over. Preston was taking photographs with his memory.

Macho came out of the kitchen with his arm Marco's sister's neck. He nodded his head to the music and brought her in front of Preston. "Say, Kid, this is Kayley. It's her party, she turns twenty tomorrow. Kayley, this is Preston. He's like my brother."

Kayley stepped in front of Preston and looked up at him. She tapped on his sunglasses. "Hello, are you in there?" Kayley was five-feet-four inches tall, dark-skinned, with a nice shape and figure. She had shoulder-length hair that was curled and soulful brown eyes.

Preston pulled his glasses off his face and couldn't stop looking at her. He had a thing for dark-skinned women, and he had never seen a more gorgeous female than Kayley. He tucked his glasses into his pocket and extended his hand. "I'm Preston, happy birthday."

She smiled and batted her eyelashes. "Well, technically it's not my birthday until tomorrow, but thank you just the same. I haven't ever seen you around before. Where are you from?" She found Preston attractive.

Ever since her father married Maria Marco's mother she had been forced to be around nothing but Puerto Ricans, and it wasn't that it bothered her, but she just had a thing for her race of men.

"I'm from Guilford, and I don't be over on this side of town for obvious reasons. How the hell is you Marco's sister and you're so chocolate?" Preston wanted to know, though he had heard that Puerto Ricans came in all colors. Kayley was brazened, she took his hand, and pulled him into the hallway away from the party.

Macho threw his arms up. “Damn, that's how y'all do me? Alright, it’s good.” He waved them off and slipped into the party so he could find Marco.

Kayley laughed and led Preston into the den, where she closed the door.

Preston looked her over. “You tryna kidnap me or something?” He watched her lock the door. His eyes drifted to her ass and saw that it was poked out like a pregnant belly.

“N’all it ain't nothing like that. My mother been married to Marco's father for two years and I still ain't mastered listening to all that damn Spanish music. I like a lot of it, but some of it gives me a headache. I just need some peace and quiet for a minute.” She sat on the soft black leather couch across from him after he sat.

“Oh, so y'all are just siblings through marriage?”

“Yeah, but Marco is my brother, and I love him. What's good with you, though?”

“What do you mean?” Preston watched her cross her legs and reveal a nice portion of her thighs. He'd been out for a few weeks and still had yet to have his physical needs met? Kayley was looking good to him.

“Well, first of all, I'm from Houston, and down there we don't hold back, and we don't sugar coat nothin’. I think that yo’ caramel ass is fine as hell. I been watching you since you came to my party. I like your set up, and how you've let one Rican broad after the next walk past you without so much as lowering your shades to get a better view of the skimpy shit that they're wearing around here. But as soon as I stepped in front of you the glasses came off altogether. That must mean that you're feeling me?"

"Damn, you peeped all that?" Preston was impressed.

"I sure did. So, now what?" She leaned forward on the couch so she could hear his response better.

Preston laughed and moved across the room until he was sitting next to her. He looked into her brown eyes. "Hell yeah, I'm feeling you. That chocolate skin killing these females at this party. These brown-eyes and these real thick thighs gotta come straight from the motherland. How could I not honor you with taking off my glasses just so I could appreciate this natural African beauty?"

Kayley laughed. "Aw, so you just gon' run the best game you got on me, huh?" She stared at him. "I already know I can't fuck with these Rican hoes. These bitches are born naturally fine. It's all good, though." She lowered her head, and a host of her new Puerto Rican friends flashed through her mind. They were all flawless to her.

"Man, fuck them bitches out there. You got my attention, right here and right now. So, what's really good? I can tell something is wrong with you." He scooted closer and absorbed the scent of her perfume, he liked it.

Kayley didn't know Preston from Adam but for some reason, she felt comfortable and safe with him. She still couldn't believe that he was giving her the time of day with so many beautiful Spanish girls roaming through the party. She'd felt so out of place ever since she'd moved from Houston with her mother Jackie.

"N'all, it's just that from time to time I feel out of place here. I miss my people. I really ain't feeling this party either. It's more for Marco than it is for me. I only know a few people here. I wish I could ditch it."

"Shid, why not? We can leave this ma'fucka, right now. Just you and me." Preston thought about the mission of getting closer to Marco for the sting and cursed. "Damn, n'all, I can't do that. Macho drove, my shit parked."

"I got a Lexus, if you're really talking about bouncing, we can roll for a few hours. I kind of just want to talk. Would you be up for that?" She lowered her head and shook it imagining a nice quiet night rolling through Baltimore. She missed Houston.

Preston tilted her chin upward. "Maybe we can do that tomorrow or something on your actual birthday. Today just let your friends celebrate you. I look forward to chilling with you, though. What's your Facebook info?"

They exchanged Facebook information before Marco began knocking on the door. Kayley got up and answered it. Marco looked down at her, then back to Preston. Preston gave him a head nod.

Marco ignored it. "Kayley, everybody is out here looking for you. Come on, there are a few people I want you to meet." He held the door open for her.

"I'll meet you in the kitchen in a split second let me say a few last words to him, and I'll be in there. Go ahead." She looked back at Preston and smiled.

Marco froze for a second. He mugged Preston, then looked back down at Kayley. "Alright sis but just hurry up. You already know.Roberto is feeling you. He's talking about buying you a Range Rover for your birthday tomorrow."

"Alright, Marco, I'll talk to you about that in a minute." She ushered him out and closed the door.

Marco took one last glance back to Preston before the door closed in his face.

Preston stepped up to Kayley and took a hold of her possessively. "Roberto?" He held her around the waist.

"Ain't nobody studyin', Roberto. But I will be rolling with you this weekend, though, right?" She stared into his brown eyes again.

"Hit me up and I'ma make you a priority. I like this crazy feeling I get from you already. I think you and I are going to be a problem together. What do you think?"

"I didn't even know we were together." She stepped on her tippy toes and wrapped her arms around his neck.

Preston slid his hands over her ass and cuffed it while he lowered his head and kissed her soft lips. Their tongues attacked one another's, then they were sucking on each other's lips loudly, breathing heavy. "I gotta have you, Kayley."

She wiped his spit from her lips and laughed. "It's crazy cause I get the same feeling." She looked him up and down one last time treasuring the scent of his rare Cologne, and shivered. "I'ma hit you up. You, betta hit me back, too."

"I will, I promise you that."

Chapter 5

It was go time, Preston adjusted his mask and frowned underneath the cloth. He held his trusted 9 mm on his side and looked over the backyard of Marco's place one more time. It was eleven o'clock at night, and Macho was sure everything was taking place at Marco's trap house where he'd held Kayley's party. Preston saw that everything appeared calm. He stood beside the back door ready to kick it in as hard as he could. They had to act fast, Marco would be on his way back with a trunk load of money from the many shipments he'd done for the Puerto Rican Syndicate that week. They wanted to rob his trap, then catch him slipping with all the cash when he returned.

Macho hopped the fence with one of his Hittas out of Guildford. He directed the Hitta to go beside Preston while he slipped beside Preston as well. Marco held a fifty round Mach-90 in his hand that he'd borrowed from one of his old heads of Guilford. He nodded his head at Preston and stood up. He slipped around to the front of the house running as low to the ground as he possibly could. When he got here, he hopped over the railing of the porch and stood in front of the door. He waited until he heard Preston kick in the back door before he kicked in the front as hard as he could.

Whoom!

He rushed inside with the Mach-90 held in front of him. "Get down! Get down! Get down muthafuckas, right now. Or I swear to God I'ma wetting you! Do it!"

There were five people that he could see in the house. Four at the table where they were bagging up large quantities of China White. Marco's eyes lit up; he was already appraising the dope. He began slinging the occupants to the floor one at a time. When they were lying face down, he began searching them and taking their weapons off them. “Tear this ma’fucka up, check everything. Go!”

Preston came into the living room with a black garbage bag. He started dumping the Heroin in the bags brick by brick. When he cleared all they visibly had he wrapped the bag in a knot, and slowly backed into the kitchen tearing the refrigerator apart just in case Marco or his people left anything inside it. Macho had told him that Marco's people had a habit of hiding things in it, but he found nothing. He rushed back toward the living room and stopped in his tracks when he came across the bedroom and saw Preston's Hitta with his gun up under Kayley's chin. He had the trigger pulled back ready to slump her.

Preston rushed into the bedroom. “What the fuck are you doing, nigga?”

“She knows who I am, she said my name.” He pointed to his shoes. “Marco bought me these. She gon’ tell him and he's going to kill my whole family. I gotta kill this bitch.” He flung Kayley to the floor and aimed his gun down at her with the intent of slaying her.

“No!” Preston pushed him as hard as he could.

The Shooter crashed into the dresser and fell to the floor. He hopped up and got ready to aim his gun at Preston. Preston lowered his eyes and popped him four times with no mercy.

Boom! Boom! Boom! Boom!

The Shooter crashed into the dresser again and fell on the floor leaking blood out of his neck and chest.

Kayley scooted as far away from the scene as she could. “Oh, my God! Oh, my God! Oh, my God!” She trembled.

“What the fuck going on back there? Tell me something!” The Shooter yelled. He kept his Mach trained on the four dope boys. He was ready to panic. He was hoping nothing had happened to Preston. “Fuck!” He knew he couldn't leave the dope boys from fear they would get up.

He closed his eyes and cursed under his breath. He aimed his Mach and began chopping them down with bullets. The gun jumped in his hands and spit out the shells. The four dope boys attempted to get up and run after they felt the hot lead entering their flesh. Before they could make it to the exit they were deceased.

Having not heard anything from Preston, Macho panicked. “Preston, where you at, bruh? Say somethin!”

Preston stuffed Kayley in the closet and covered her with coats. “Don't say shit, baby, please. If you do, we gon’ have to kill you. Let me take care of this, I got you. Okay?”

Kayley nodded. “Okay.” She didn't know why he was choosing to help her, but she was thankful that he was. “Thank you, Preston. I owe you, I swear I do.”

Preston paused for a second and grew weary. A prison bed crossed his mind and he had second thoughts about letting Kayley walk away unscathed, but then something in his heart told him he could trust her. “Alright, be smooth and not a word.” He covered her up. “Bruh, let's get the fuck out of here!”

Macho rushed into the room and saw his Hitta laid out on the floor. “What the fuck happened to him?” He watched the fluid ooze out of his Shooter's chest. His eyes were wide open as if he was still in shock, but he was long gone from life.

Preston waved him off. “It’s a long story. Come on, we gotta catch Marco before he makes it back here.” Preston ran out of the room.

Macho stood there for a second lost. They had come into the house to pull a simple robbery and were leaving five bodies behind, one of them that included his lil’ homie. He sighed, bent over and grabbed the Shooter's pistol from beside his body. He closed his eyes out of respect, then bounced out of the house behind Preston in confusion.

***

Marco leaned his seat slightly back and unzipped his pants. He pulled his dick out and looked over at Marika. Marika was his baby mother, Marsha's little sister. Marika was trying to make a splash amongst the other dope girls from Wilson street. He was her connect, and whenever he could get her from around Marsha, he took full advantage of her. "Handle me, Marika."

Marika licked her juicy pink lips, took out her bubble gum and placed it in the ashtray. "I got you, Papi." She leaned across the console and took a hold of his pipe. Seconds later her mouth slid up and down it in a fast motion.

Marco grunted and adjusted himself in his seat to give her better access. He waited for the light to turn green before he stepped on the gas. He drove with his eyes lowered. Marika made loud sucking noises that were driving him crazy. She popped him out and licked all over the head, then suck on it hard. He found himself moaning under his breath.

She popped him out again. "You like that, Papi?"

Marco grunted again. "Hell yeah. Do your thing, Mami."

She stroked him faster and licked all around his head. "Marco, pull over up there. I don't want you to crash. Plus, I want you to hit this pussy when I get you nice and hard. Can you do that for lil' sissy?" She unbuttoned her blouse to show him the swelling of her breasts.

Marco shivered, Marika mighta been young but she was always ready and about that action. Having her strong Puerto Rican features, and sista built body she was a sight to behold. At only eighteen-years-old, Marco was sure that she was set to be a force to be reckoned with. He was glad he had her locked down and under his thumb. He pulled over on Parker Place and cut the engine. The block was dark and deserted. It was a one-way street, and the apartments there were basically packed with senior citizen tenants.

Marika sucked him back into her mouth and went hard bobbing her head like a pro. She slurped loudly and rubbed his piece all over her lips. “Alright, Papi, now I wanna ride that ma’fucka.” She inched her skirt up and opened her thighs wide so he could see her freshly shaved pussy lips. She ran a finger through them to separate her folds. “I know you can't wait to get back into this tight baby, right here, can you?” She squeezed his dick hard.

Precum oozed out of the head. He whimpered, “Bitch, get up here.” He leaned the seat all the way back and took his piece from her stroking it.

Marika giggled and came across the car's console. She climbed on top of him and found his dick with her left hand. She moved it from side to side playing with her petals, then slowly sunk down on it feeling him with her wet heat. He stretched her the further she slid down him. When she was sitting on his balls, she took a hold of the headrest and slowly rode him sucking on his neck.

“Mmm! Mmm! Marco, you're fucking your baby mother's little sister again,” she whispered in Spanish. “She ever finds out, she gon’ kill us.” Her tight snatch gripped him as she bounced up and down harder.

Marco didn't care who she was to Marsha. He'd been fucking Marika since she was sixteen and couldn't see himself shying away from her anytime soon. As far he was concerned, she belonged to him just as much as her sister did. He bit into her neck and took ahold of her little hips forcing her to ride him harder and faster. The truck rocked back and forth on its suspensions. The windows quickly fogged up from all the heavy breathing. Marco opened her blouse to reveal her perky breasts. He squeezed them, and thumbed her nipples, before pinching them while she screamed and rode him with reckless abandonment.

"We're so wrong, Marco! Uh! Uh! Shit, we're so wrong!" She popped back as far as she could, then forward with equal intensity.

Marco held her ass and relished in the feel of her hot insides. He leaned his head forward to suck her erect nipples. "I love this pussy! I love it!"

Crash!

The driver's side window exploded causing Marika to scream and fall off Marco's lap. A masked Preston reached through the window and grabbed a hand full of Marco's hair pulling him through it. He dropped him to the ground and placed the .45 that Macho had taken off the slain Shooter to his head.

"Bitch ass nigga don't move. Be absolutely still or I'm smoking you."

Marco laid on his back with his eyes bucked wide open. His pants were around his waist, and he was so shocked and embarrassed that he was frozen in place. "Say, Pa Pa, I know this is a robbery. I ain't tryna play wit' you. You can take the five stacks I got in my pocket and go. I don't want no trouble."

A masked Macho stepped over him and kicked him in the chin knocking him out cold. He stuck his head in the car and eyed Marika closely. "Lil' mama, hand me them keys, right there. Did you make sure that he loaded that bitch up?"

Marika took the keys out of the ignition and handed them to Macho. She nodded. "It's supposed to be fifty thousand. At least that's what I heard him say on the phone."

Macho nodded. “Get yo ass out of this car and run to the nearest business and get help. I'ma hit you up later. Daddy, promise okay?”

“Okay, Daddy.” She hopped out of the car, pulled down her skirt and followed his orders accordingly. She ran full feed to the nearest gas station.

Macho popped the trunk and removed the duffel bag full of cash. He kneeled on the ground and unzipped it. When he looked inside and saw that it was filled with bills, he opened it wide enough for Preston to see it as well. He zipped it back up and hurried back to his awaiting Jeep that was parked in the alley.

Preston stood a slight distance from Marco's car. He aimed his gun and finger fucked the trigger chopping his car up as much as he could. He wanted the job to be made to look as if it were personal. After busting out all the windows. He took off running full speed behind Macho.

Chapter 6

"You see I told you, I was going to make sure my little girl was taken care of. You gotta stop doubting me, LaShawn." Pooh stopped in front of his black Yukon Denali and opened the door for Lashonda to get in the back. Once she was in, he stuffed her ten shopping bags inside the truck with her. He placed all the bags around her to make her feel like a six-year-old bosset.

LaShawn felt like she had a headache coming on full-fledged. She rubbed her temples as she sat in the passenger seat of the truck. "Pooh, if you made it a habit of doing this kind of thing on a regular basis, I wouldn't have the room to doubt you. You do this every so often, then you make this girl think you are some sort of hero. This shit gets old."

Pooh make sure, Lashonda was strapped in tightly inside her booster seat. He kissed her cheek and slammed the back door. He looked over his shoulder at Lashonda once he was sitting in the driver's seat of his whip. "Baby, put your headphones on for a minute so me and mommy can talk."

"But, Daddy, y'all aren't about to argue you are y'all?" Lashonda was hoping they weren't about to ruin such a good day with their senseless arguing.

"Just put your headphones on Lashonda or I'ma take away that iPad," LaShawn threatened.

"No, you ain't. I brought her that. You ain't about to take nothing from my lil' girl that I brought her," he scoffed. "Baby, do what Daddy says."

"Okay." Lashonda fixed the headphones over her ears and started up her iPad.

"Lashonda? Lashonda?" Pooh called trying to see if she had followed his directions. When he saw that she had he turned to LaShawn. "Bitch, why you always gotta start some shit every time I'm trying to do something right with my daughter?"

"First of all, Pooh, don't be calling me out of my name. I ain't yo' bitch. My name is, LaShawn, thank you very much."

"Like I said, bitch why you always gotta start some shit with me when I am trying to do something right with my baby. You're one of them scorned, bum ass, baby mamas ain't you?"

LaShawn was so shocked that he had come at her so hard, she damn near choked on her spit. "Excuse yo' muthafuckin' self?" She could feel herself becoming angry and highly emotional. She couldn't understand how any man could talk to the mother of their child the way Pooh did her. It made her feel so low and worthless. She hated that she gave him so much of her power.

"Bitch, you heard me. You are one of those bum ass, baby mothers who mad because they couldn't lock down a boss nigga like me. I'm sitting here dripping in sauce, and yo' punk ass flooded in bills. That shit ain't my fault. I'm doing my part for Lashonda and Lashonda only. Fuck you thought, I was supposed to take you shopping or somethin', too?" He started the ignition and grabbed his pistol from under the driver's seat, putting it on his lap as he mugged her.

"Pooh, you, betta watch yo' mouth with how talk to me. I ain't called you out of your name one time. And I don't need you to take me shopping. I am an independent woman. Always have been, always will be."

"Independent my ass. Yo', word is bond, if I find out you been on some unfit shit with my daughter, I'm taking her away from yo' ass asap. She shouldn't be living in that busted ass duplex no damn way when her father is getting ready to buy a fuckin' palace." He thought it was necessary to jack on LaShawn as much as possible. She always gave him a look that made him feel that he wasn't a major nigga like he felt he was. It was like she could see through his facade all the way to his inner boy that yearned to be accepted and set apart from mediocre dudes in the game.

"Look, Pooh, I don't know what you're getting at, but I have not now, nor will I ever be unfit to my child. I appreciate you for taking her shopping today, but boy don't let this shit blow your head up. It's only your responsibility to keep her straight until I can meet you halfway there. I'm down, right now, but I'll get there. I won't be broke forever. I'm recently laid off, but I'll figure it out real soon."

"It sho' is taking yo' ass a long time, though. That's why I only fuck wit' boss bitches. You bum hoes be taking up space. Word up." He shook his head and turned his nose up at her. "Yo', I'm finna take my baby out to eat. If you ain't got no money you gon' have to wait in the car until we get back unless you want me to drop you off at a bus stop, right now."

"What, are you serious?" LaShawn popped the locks on her passenger's door ready to get out.

"As a heart attack. It ain't for me to trick my dick on you. This is pimping, Shorty. You got some money you can roll. If you're broke, then bitch I'ma have to fuck with you later when I drop her off."

LaShawn was over him, she opened the passenger's door. "You know what, you ain't gotta worry about us finding a way home we'll get there. She opened the back door. "Come on, Lashonda we're leaving."

"I can't hear you, mommy." Lashonda pointed to her headphones.

LaShawn reached into the back of the truck and pulled them off her head. "I said, we are leaving. Now let's go."

Pooh stepped out of the truck and closed his driver's side door. The bright sunlight reflected off his forehead. There was barely any breeze flowing through the atmosphere. He walked around the truck until he was standing beside LaShawn. "Yo' stop playing wit' me, LaShawn. It's my weekend with her, and she ain't going nowhere. This is my ma'fuckin' daughter, too."

LaShawn grabbed ahold of Lashonda's hand. "Pooh, when you learn how to respect me as her mother then we'll talk about your rights to her. Until then you can move so we can be on our way." She got ready to go inside the truck so she could release Lashonda from her booster seat and seat belts.

Pooh nudged her to the side as inconspicuous as he could. He pulled her away from the truck and closed the door. He wiped his mouth with his hands. He was vexed. "Yo', on my moms, I'm tired of you playing wit' me about my kid. You keep fucking wit' me and I'ma make yo' ass pay over my, shorty. Now I'm trying to be humble." He adjusted the pistol in his waistband. He looked both ways to see how many witnesses were out.

LaShawn was no dummy. She got his drift and didn't want to play wit' her safety. "Look, Pooh, all I want is to take Lashonda home. You can get her tomorrow. Today ain't gon' work, though." She stared at the ground instead of at him.

"Bitch, fuck tomorrow. You betta get yo' punk ass on or on my word I'ma stank you about my seed. The courts say I got her until Monday at seven. Bitch, I'll see you on Monday at seven and not a day or a minute earlier. Bye." He mugged her for a second and slid his hand under his shirt grasping the handle of his gun.

He surveyed the scene again. There were ten other people inside the shopping plaza. He was irritated. Had they not been there he woulda popped LaShawn and kept it moving. He was overall the drama that came with her already.

LaShawn backed up. "Okay, Pooh, it's all good." She kept her eyes on the spot where his right hand fumbled with the handle of the gun. "Just please bring my baby back safely. Don't have her around all of them ratchet dope boys. Please."

"Bitch, bye! She wit' me for a few days. I know how to take care of my lil' girl. Go get yo' broke ass on the bus." He got into his Denali and pulled away from the curb loudly.

LaShawn chased after his truck for thirty seconds and stopped breathing hard. Her eyes misted over and ran down her cheeks. She prayed that she would see Lashonda again safe and sound. Besides Preston, she felt like her daughter was all that she really had.

***

Macho rolled to the stoplights of Martin Luther King Drive with his head nodding to the *Tee Grizzley* track bumping out of his speakers when he saw a disheveled LaShawn standing at the bus stop. She looked sick, he scanned the neighborhood and knew that where they currently were, was frivolous for drive-bys and shootouts. The neighborhood was infested with Heroin and methamphetamine. The dashboard told him it was 6:15, and there was only an hour left of daylight. He didn't know when the bus would come, and he wasn't about to leave her behind knowing what type of dude Preston was.

Preston would never leave one of his loved ones out in a bad neighborhood, he was sure of that. He made a U-turn and pulled up alongside LaShawn. He tapped the horn twice and rolled down his passenger's window. "Shorty, what you on?"

"Nothing, I'm about to head home. I've had a rough day." She stepped to the curb and looked down the street to see if she could locate the bus. She was nervous about being on King Drive after dark and prayed the city bus showed up soon so she wouldn't have too. They were running forty-five minutes apart.

"Man, stop playing wit' me. I ain't about to let you stay on no bus stop. Get in, I'ma take you home," Macho called.

"Macho, I'm good. Go ahead on your way. The bus should be coming in a little while." She looked down the street again. There was a group of dope addicts posted up across the street from her. They looked over at her with lust in their eyes. She became nervous.

"Yo', don't make me get out of this car, LaShawn. Damn, just roll with me, I got you." Macho mugged the niggas across the street.

He saw how they were looking over at LaShawn and threw his Jeep in park. He grabbed his pistol from the console and cocked it. Then threw open the door and jogged across the street. He waited for one car to roll past before he made it to the group's side of the street.

"Fuck y'all looking at her for like y'all about to take somethin'? Shit ain't sweet, bitch niggas move." He raised the gun in the air and bucked four loud shots.

Bocka! Bocka! Bocka! Bocka!

The group took off running at full speed. He tucked his gun and walked back across the street. "Let's go, LaShawn, I ain't gon' ask yo' ass again."

LaShawn hurried to the Jeep and got inside of it. "Damn, boy, you so crazy. Why did you do that?"

Macho pulled away from the curb. "Because I ain't like the way they was looking at you. These niggas over here are known for being rapists and all kinds of shit. That ain't happening with you. Word up." His eyebrows were furrowed.

LaShawn was quiet for a moment. She really didn't know what to say. It had been a long time since any man outside of Preston had acted as if they actually cared about her safety and wellbeing. "Thank you for caring, Macho, but you really don't have to."

"Yes, I do. I know you ain't fucking with me on that level, but you already know how I feel about you and have since day one." He looked over at her. "You know it's supposed to be me and you, LaShawn."

LaShawn suddenly felt hot and bothered. "I don't know what you mean?" She avoided his eyes. "You already know how, Preston, would feel about that. When he first introduced us, he said he never wanted to find out that you and I had even spoken behind his back. So, you already know anything more than that is a no go. That's why I've never entertained that thought."

"Yeah, well I have, and I still am. Preston is my nigga, but I'm grown and so are you. I ain't never seen a woman badder than you, LaShawn. I ain't never seen a better mother either. I know that fuck nigga, Pooh, been taking you through it. I'd waste his punk ass if he wasn't your kid's father. But even so, I want you for myself. I know, I can be that man for you, and Lashonda. I mean probably not, right now, but real soon. You know once I get my bands up. I know I gotta have a bag in order to fuck in yo' bidness."

She smiled. "Nall it ain't nothing like that. I am an independent woman, I can hold my own. I'm just going through a rough patch, right now. Things will get better, and when it does everybody gon' know it because they will see a new me."

"But what happens if they are already in love with the old you, or the, right now you?"

LaShawn blushed and looked out of the window. "Boy." She shook her head. "I done heard about you. They say that both you and Preston's heart are cold as ice. Y'all scary."

"Not for you my heart ain't. I'm feeling you, and I got a huge place in my heart for you and Lashonda. All I need is for you to give me that chance. I promise I won't fail you."

"But what about, Preston?" she asked and finally looked over at him. She wanted to see the expression on his face as he explained himself.

He shrugged his shoulders. "That's my nigga, but he don't set no rules for me. He as a man should be happy that a good man is willing to hold his sister down like no other. That's exactly what I would do."

"And my baby daddy drama, what about that? You already know, Pooh is a handful." She imagined what he'd just done to her about Lashonda and it made her angry.

"Far as I'm concerned, I'll body that nigga, right now if you give me the go-ahead. I don't like him or nothin' he stands for. But until you do, I'll be respectful and follow your lead. I just wanna make you happy," he meant it.

"Dang, Macho, you're messing with my head. I didn't even know you were feeling me like that. Can you give me some time to think about this before you dismiss me?"

Macho was serious. "I would never dismiss you. Maybe we should just start slow and take it from there?"

"You mean like friends?" She wanted him to clarify just so she could get the best understanding.

"Nall, I don't believe that men and women can be friends. I mean you and I could maybe start the dating process out slow with no strings attached at first. How does that sound?" He pulled in front of her place on Liberty Avenue.

LaShawn was secretly irritated that they had gotten to her house so fast. She was liking his company. "That sounds cool, Macho. Why don't you slide into my DM and we'll see what's good?"

Now Macho laughed and smiled. “Be careful talking like that, or you gon’ get me in trouble right away.”

LaShawn blushed for what felt like the hundredth time. “Yeah, get your mind out of the gutter.” She sighed. “Well, I guess, I'll hear from you later. You be safe out here.” She opened the passenger door.

Macho pulled her to him and kissed her lips with so much passion that she moaned. She closed her eyes and kissed him back. Her right hand rested on the side of his face as they appreciated each other orally. Macho rubbed her side until her shirt lifted just enough for him to feel her hot waist. His hand traveled under her shirt and found the front of her bra. LaShawn licked his lips and sucked on them.

He squeezed her hard nipple lightly. She moaned and thrust her chest at him. Then she broke the kiss and hopped out of the Jeep. She stood beside the Jeep out of breath. She was embarrassed at her behavior. She waved to him, before jogging up on her porch, and going inside the house. She closed the door with her back to it. She took a second to gather herself. Her head tilted to the ceiling. She laughed and felt a whole lot better.

‘*Macho is something else,*’ she thought while replaying their entire conversation in her mind.

Macho sat staring at LaShawn's home. He was rock hard and feenin' for her. Something told him to knock on the door, pick her up and go in on her. But he lacked the nerve, instead, he pulled off determined to make her his.

Chapter 7

"I'm surprised, you're actually meeting me, this better not be no type of set up." Preston slid into the passenger's seat of Kayley's two thousand and twenty Lexus truck. He'd already checked the back seat and circled the block a few times before he got inside.

"What type of woman would I be? You saved my life two weeks ago, then I come and set you up. That would be bogus as hell." She drove away from the curb into the night.

It was seven o'clock on a Thursday night. The streets of Baltimore appeared relatively calm. There was a light drizzle coming down from the sky. Kayley turned on her windshield wipers and looked over at Preston. He smelled so good to her.

"What made you wait two weeks before you hit me up?" He wanted to pick her brain a little bit. When it came to females in Baltimore you could never be too careful. They would set you up faster than a dude would have.

"You really wanna know?" She side-eyed him.

"Yeah, tell me what's good." He ran his tongue up and down a Garcia Vega blunt that he'd stuffed with Kush.

"Even though I don't know you that well my spirit was missing you. I felt like I needed to be in your presence. That's why I hit you up, and that's why we're rolling, right now." She smiled. "You got anymore questions?"

Preston didn't know what to make of her comment, so he ignored it enough to try and come up with a response for it later. For now, he felt there were more pressing matters. "What's good with that fool, Marco? Do he suspect it's us?"

"I don't know. Ever since all that stuff happened the police has been all over his places, and Wilson street. Marco has been tooting powder like crazy, and he just hasn't been himself. I think he suspects everybody, and the worst thing about it all is that the people he was in business with are demanding their money, and dope. They have him a thirty-day deadline to get it back or they promise a bloodbath on Wilson Street. I don't know if Marco will be able to fulfill their requests. So, I've been avoiding Wilson street altogether, it's scary." She tightened her left fist on the wheel. "Can I ask you something, Preston? You don't have to answer it if you don't want too. But I would really like to know?"

"What's that?"

"Why did you guys choose to rob him, and more importantly why did you stop that guy from killing me?"

"So, you got two questions then?" He kept looking out the passenger's window. He was slumped low in his seat with his hand under his shirt. He didn't know how far he could trust Kayley and giving her the benefit of the doubt had his stomach in knots. "Well, I can't answer the first question because business is business. The second question is simple, you my sista, and that shit ain't have nothing to do with you. I ain't finna let nobody waste one of my people when they're innocent."

"Oh."

"What's the matter, why you say oh like that?" He looked over at her.

"Aw, because I was just hoping it was a little more than that. I thought you have been feeling a way about me. But I shoulda known. I got that hopeless romantic stuff in me real bad, it's actually borderline insanity." She laughed nervously hoping she hadn't said too much.

"Yeah, and I got this tough man shit in me too much as well. I hate feeling all soft and shit but I'ma keep it real. I saved you because I like you. I wasn't about to let that bitch ass nigga kill you when I done barely got the chance to know you. I woulda never been able to sleep. Besides, this shit was about Marco's money and dope, not about his sister by marriage."

"So, then you did save me because you were feeling a way about me?" Kayley perked up.

"Yeah, I guess you can say that. And if this was one of those Lifetime movies you would be in my debt," he teased her, although he was serious.

"Oh, yeah, and just what would it take in order for me to get out of your debt if I was in it?" She pulled to a stoplight and looked over at him. The rain beaded down on her windshield full blast now. The light drizzle had become a full-fledged thunderstorm.

"I'm just saying, I'm the only one that ain't got a chance to give the birthday girl nothing for her birthday. What's really good?" He eyed her thick thighs that were just outside of her Nine West skirt. Her chocolate skin appealed to him in a way that drove him crazy.

"I ain't been with nobody since I been over here from Houston. I ain't feeling these Rican men like that. It's something about you, Preston, I think I want you."

Preston slid his hand on to her right thigh. He was already rock hard. "I need you, Kayley. I promise to God I do."

***

Kayley opened the door to her apartment, just as Preston picked her up and carried her inside. He kicked the door closed and crashed into the wall with her. She moaned as he sucked on her neck and licked along the length of it. He held her up by holding her ass under the skirt. She was wearing a thong, so her cheeks felt hot in his palms.

"Tell me that you want me, Kayley. I need to hear that shit." He bit into her neck and sucked hard.

"Uhhh, I want you, Preston. Damn, I want you. I don't be doing shit like this." She closed her eyes and tilted her head back.

Preston lowered her to the carpet. He yanked her skirt up aggressively and exposed her things underneath. He took the cloth and pulled it upward until her panties formed a meaty camel toe. He kissed her directly on the center of her panties and sucked her lips one at a time through the material.

"I wanna eat this pussy, Kayley. Ever since I saw yo' lil' thick, chocolate ass I been wanting to eat yo' pussy." He rubbed her sex through the panties.

Kayley opened her thighs as wide as they could go giving him access to her charms. "Eat this pussy then, Preston. Welcome me to Baltimore the right way, do it." Her tongue traced her mouth, she was in heat.

Preston yanked the panties to the side and sniffed her pussy. He inhaled the aroma and opened the chocolate lips to reveal her glossy bubble gum center. He shivered at its sight. "Ain't nothing like black pussy. I swear to God I love my sistas." He licked up and down her crease slurping her juices along the way.

Kayley arched her back. "Uhhh, shit!"

Preston's tongue was a blur as it traced up and down her center and ran circles around her clit. He sucked on the nub and nipped at it with his teeth lightly. She screamed and humped into his mouth. She grabbed the back of his head and forced him to eat her some more. He complied hungrily, munching and swallowing everything that came out of her.

"Preston, you doing too much. Uhhh! You doing too much!" She felt his lips trap her clitoris, then he was sucking again. She came, stuffing his face into her pussy while she rode it popping her back.

Preston breathed through his nose. He slurped, sucked and flicked her clit until she pushed him away. Then he stood up and dropped his shorts and boxers. His big dick flopped in the air. He kneeled down between her thighs and pulled her to him aggressively. Her pussy lips were already slightly parted from his sucking. Cream oozed out of her, and down to her ass cheeks.

He took the head of his pipe and rubbed it all in her juices before sliding into her slit. She held her lips open for him. Slowly his piece slipped in her, widening her gash and filling her up at the same time. She opened her mouth wide in shock at the feel of him stuffing her. She fell to the carpet and squeezed her breasts together. Preston helped her take off her blouse. Next, her bra was removed. Her chocolate breasts were revealed to his eyes. He trembled and began to long stroke her squeezing her titties.

"Aw shit. Aw shit. Unnhh! Unnhh! Aw shit. Yes! Yes, Preston! Fuck me, Daddy!" She wrapped her thick thighs around his waist and allowed him to pound her out with no mercy.

Preston loved the way her hotness squeezed his pole. She was super wet. It sounded like he was smacking his hand into a puddle of water. He leaned down and sucked her neck. "This pussy good. Fuck! This pussy good! Unnhh, shit!" He rolled his back digging deeper and deeper, fucking her harder and harder on his savage shit.

Kayley sat up and pulled him down on top of her. She kissed and licked all over his lips. Her nails dig into his sides while he fucked her. She held her mouth open again struggling to breathe. Preston licked all around her lips and sucked her bottom one into his mouth while he pounded with deeper thrusts. She opened her legs wide and locked them back around him. "Awww fuck!" Her eyes rolled into the back of her head. She dug her nails into his shoulder blades.

Preston growled like an angry Lion ready to kill its vulnerable prey. He began to shudder as he felt his orgasm mounting. "I'm finna cum, Kayley. Shit, I'm—finna—cum!" He balled her up and stroked her as fast as he could cumming in large jets.

His back jerked over and over. He thought about what he was doing and the consequences it could have and pulled out. His cum flew out of him, all over her chocolate pussy lips. He opened her open and finished cumming on her pink.

Kayley ran her thumb around her clit until she screamed. "Shit, I'm cumming again. I'm cumming again!" She laid back and squirted her cum at him while she rubbed her clit furiously. She opened her sex lips wider and spit again into the air.

Preston took a hold of her clit and rubbed it furiously. He pinched it and blew on it. She skeeted some more and over backward kicking at him. He laughed and sucked his fingers. "Hell yeah, this what I'm talking about."

***

After their shower, Kayley laid on his chest and rubbed up and down his stomach. He had a bit of a gut and she liked it. She kissed his neck. "Preston, I think I'm falling for you way too fast. I don't like feeling like this already."

Preston was exhausted. He moved his pillow slightly to get comfortable and make sure he could grab his pistol from under it when he needed too. "Yo', as crazy as it may seem I'm feeling crazy over yo' as already, too. I can tell you're about to be my lady and I ain't about to play about you."

Kayley hugged him tighter. "What that mean?"

“That means that it’s about to be us. Fuck Wilson Street. You're about to be under me, and only me.” He moved her so that she was straddled on top of him. “You hear what I said?”

“Aw, you think it’s gon’ be that easy to lock me down?” She looked into his eyes daringly.

“You muthafuckin’ right. I'm staking my claim, right now. You Kayley, belong to me.”

“Den you belong to me too den. This ain't no one-way street. If you ain't about to play about me I ain't finna play ‘bout you either. So, what you got to say about that?” She reached between them and slid back onto his erect piece. She engulfed him slowly heating him up and groaned.

It was Preston's turn for his eyes to roll into the back of his head. He gasped and jumped upward to drive himself deeper into her body. “I'm wit' it. Umm! Umm! Umm! It’s official.”

“Yeah, it’s official.” She stopped riding him and slid all the way down on his pole. “It’s official, it’s us from here on out.” She slid down his body dislodging his piece and sucked it into her mouth. “I'm about to show you some Southern hospitality right quick.” She sucked her juices off him and went to work like an animal.

Chapter 8

It was three weeks later, Preston stood in front of Macho at St. Helena park on Willow Springs Road directly in the heart of the slums of Baltimore. It was a hot and sunny afternoon, with no breeze. The sun was blazing, it was ninety degrees outside, and Preston was already irritated. He wiped the sweat from his forehead and eyed the twenty young killas that stood behind Macho. Six of them were females, and all of them were dressed in some form of red. Preston already knew what that was about. Macho stepped closer to him and wrapped his left arm around Preston's neck taking him away from the crowd of hungry killas.

"Yo', before you even say somethin' crazy, Preston. I need for you to hear me out," Macho started.

"Yeah, because you already know I was finna get on yo ass. Fuck all these niggas doing here? You said I was about to meet the family. I thought that meant your actual family." Preston looked over his shoulder again.

The group of youngsters seemed to be mugging him with hatred, though it was nothing like that. All of them were hot, and all of them could sense that Preston wasn't feeling them. Macho had already told them Preston was his right-hand man. That he needed his head nod before they moved forward with anything, so the majority of them were nervous about their impending livelihood.

"Nigga, Dundalk wide open right now, and who better to cease this hood than us?" Macho began. He stopped walking with Preston and stood in place.

"What?" Preston turned to look at him. "What the fuck are you talking about?"

"Most of them Payroll Boys got indicted a few weeks back, it's only a few of them left and they ain't on shit. That leaves Dundalk wide open. I wanna step into this turf with these Slime Killas and take this bitch over some cutthroat shit. It's plenty of money to be made out here, and I got a plug out the Midwest that's looking to fuck with us on some major weight. I'm talking more than a few bricks, and this shit supposed to be potent enough to knock a mafuckas socks off. If we do it right, we can get rich in a year."

Preston was confused, and a bit dismayed. "Nigga, when did you put all this together, and when did you figure all this shit out?" He turned around to look at the group again. Some of them mugged him, while others acted like they didn't see him looking at them.

"That's all I been thinking about, Preston. Ever since we got that lil' bread from Marco I been hustling and getting my paper up. I been feeding these lil' hungry killas with the chews and few I done came up with, and they been returning the favor by any and every means. Now I'm thinking bigger, and more work. Now I need you to have my back on this, but I can respect it if you won't. Either way I gotta make shit happen Dundalk is up for grabs."

As he was finishing this sentence, Pooh and twelve of his Payroll Killas rolled up in drop-top midnight blue Porsches. Pooh jumped out of the driver's seat of the Porsche that led the pack. He was rocking a blue and black Chanel No. 9 outfit over blue and white Jordans. He had a blue bandana around his neck. He stepped into the park. His homies followed behind him.

Macho's young savages rushed from the gate and stood behind him. They slid their hands under their shirts clutching the toolies that he'd copped them for the low. Macho stepped up to Pooh and lowered his eyelids into slits. He thought about LaShawn and some of her confessions to him about Pooh and he wanted to pop him. "Nigga, what y'all want? Can't you see we in this bitch having a meeting?"

Pooh laughed. "Yeah, we see that, and that shit over with. Us Payroll niggas got business we need to discuss and we wanna chill in our park to talk about it." He looked over his shoulder at his soldiers, then back at Macho.

"Look, nigga, I don't know what the fuck you think this is? But you, niggas, ain't running shit around this mafucka. Now like I said me and my crew discussing bidness. Y'all gotta move around or else." He moved his hand closer to the small of his back where his Glock .40 was at the ready, cocked and loaded.

Pooh snickered. "Yo', Kid, word to the Gods, this ain't what you want. My advice to you, since you fuck with Preston and all that, is to quit while you're ahead. Now everybody knows this park belongs to Payroll. Y'all need to fall in line."

Now Preston was heated. He already hated Pooh. Had there not been so many witnesses around he woulda dropped him with a series of bullets. He stepped into his face. "Nigga, we don't fall in line for fuck niggas like you. Bitch nigga, you heard what the fuck my homie said. We in this bitch. Gang-gang, you ma'fuckas roll out."

"Nigga, what?" Pooh stepped in Preston's face.

Macho caught Pooh with a right hook so fast that even he didn't know he did it. He dropped him with one punch and began stomping him in the ground. "This is Cutthroat shit now. Pussy! Ass! Nigga!" He kicked and stomped him over and over while his guys watched at gunpoint.

Macho's young crew and Preston all had their burners pointed at the Payroll dope boys until Macho was finished stomping Pooh into a bloody pulp. Pooh finally got up and took off running full speed away with blood running down his neck from his mouth and nose. Macho ran to the jeep and pulled out his new Draco. He aimed it at the sky and let off a hundred shots rapidly announcing that he and Preston's crew of Cutthroats were moving into Dundalk with a vengeance.

***

That night Preston sat on the windowsill of a black nineteen-eighty-seven Chevy Caprice Classic as he and ten other cars filled up with the Cutthroat Killas slowly rolled down the block of Colgate where the few members of the Payroll dope boys' trap houses resided. He held a Mach .90 with eighty shots in the clip. His driver was sixteen and hungry for a title in the Cutthroat army. Across the hood of the car was another Shooter, he was fifteen and heartless. His whole family was starving, and he was their only hope at consistent meals each night. Preston and Macho presented new optimism in that endeavor, and he was down to pledge his undying loyalty to them.

Macho walked down the block with a Mac-1 in one hand, and a Mac-10 in the other. Behind him were four young female killas with their faces fully covered in red bandanas. Macho stopped in front of Pooh's trap, raised both street sweepers, and pulled their triggers.

Boom! Boom! Boom! Boom!

His crew followed his lead and bussed their guns chopping at the targeted houses. He sprayed with no mercy and no remorse. The windows of their houses exploded. The dope boys inside them fell to the floor and covered their heads, along with the bus downs they had with them for recreational purposes. Women screamed and the Cutthroats kept shooting.

Preston hopped out of the Chevy with a blowtorch in his hand. One of their killas ran ahead of him and doused a few of the houses with gasoline. He sparked them ablaze and walked to the next property and did the same thing. Their killas kept shooting. Preston lit a total of six properties on fire before he jumped back into the stolen Chevy firing his cannon.

Macho and his crew of females chopped at the Payroll Boys' traps, emptying their clips. They made haste back to their vehicles and stormed away from the scene leaving a red rag stuffed into Pooh's Porsche that had been shredded with bullets. Macho was geeked up, he craved a war. He knew that only the hungriest killa survived, and deep down he was exactly that and so was Preston.

***

LaShawn took two steps and slipped into Macho's arms three hours later. They were at People's Nightclub located right off Ventura Street. The club was dimly lit. The music was *India Arie*, her ballad *'Steady Love'*, blasted through the speakers. LaShawn held Macho's muscular frame tighter. She laid her head on his chest. “This feels nice.”

Macho ran his hands up and down the slope of her feminine back appreciating her curves. He was enamored by the shapely LaShawn. “Yo’, any time I get to spend with you is nice for me. I been missing you all day like crazy. Word up.” Visions of stomping out Pooh crossed his mind. Then came those of his Choppas blasting in his hands. He smiled and began to shake just a bit. He hoped she didn't notice.

“You're fa real. You were missing me like that?” She was in disbelief.

“Yeah, I miss you all the time. I be feeling incomplete as hell whenever I ain't with you.” He kissed her neck and turned her so that her back was to him. She scooted her ass into his lap and grinded from side to side. Macho got hard right away. He wanted some of LaShawn so bad.

LaShawn felt how hard his dick was, and ground into it. “I appreciate you for being so patient with me. I know you probably ain't never waited to screw a female for a whole month. Have you?”

He laughed. “You ain't just any female, LaShawn, you're that deal. When you know somethin’ is meant to be forever, you'll wait for it for as long as it takes. I know who you are, and what you're supposed to be to me. I ain't in no rush.” His dick throbbed giving him away just a little bit.

She laughed. “It seems like you are to me.”

He sucked on her neck and flicked her ear lobe with his tongue. “I am feenin' for you, though. You're so mafuckin’ fine. I love this body, and I'm crazy about you. I almost kilt that nigga today thinking about all the shit, he done did to you. Word is bond I saw myself putting his bitch ass in a casket.”

LaShawn turned around and draped her arms around his neck while she grooved with him. “I heard my baby daddy block got shot up and set on fire today. It’s been all over the news and Facebook. They were saying that they are thinking some terrorists got a hold of his neighborhood, don't tell me that was you?”

“Alright then I won't, but let's change the subject right now.” He kissed her lips. “I would love to talk about how beautiful you look in this dress which by the way is flawless.”

“Thank you, baby. Now, what did you do?” She popped his chest and walked off the dance floor.

Macho never took his eyes off her plump backside. Her ass jiggled with each step she took. Macho was mesmerized. They slid into a booth in the back of the club. Macho placed his left arm around her neck. “Look, if we gon’ start this thing off right, then I ain't gon’ hold no secrets back from you. First, I need to know if I can trust you, though?”

She nodded. “That rat shit ain't in my DNA. I am a closed safe.”

“Bet that. Yo’, I sweated that nigga, Pooh today and his entire Payroll crew. I stomped his bitch ass out after I dropped him with a right hook. Then let his hood feel how us Cutthroat niggas really get down. My word I kept seeing your pretty face and I wanted to snuff that nigga on the strength of you. Every time I see that nigga all I think about is your hurt and the pain he caused you. That shit gets me vexed. My moms went through the same shit with my father until he beat her senseless right in front of me. That's why I be crushing coward ass niggas. Word up.” His blood pressure rose from thinking about his childhood.

LaShawn turned to look into his eyes, she rubbed his face. “Baby, I'm strong. You don't have to fight my battles for me. I am a woman and we are the strongest creatures on earth. I do appreciate you, though, but I don't want you getting yourself in any trouble on the strength of me.” She kissed his lips.

“LaShawn, I love you!” As soon as the words left his mouth, he felt naked. He was supposed to be a killa, not so soft that he'd fall in love with a woman without getting the pussy first. But he couldn't help it. He had to speak from his heart. He knew she would reject him, and he was okay with it.

“What did you just say, Macho?” She backed up so she could see his face more clearly.

“I said I love you, and I don't give a fuck if it’s only been a month. I been crazy about you since day one, and I'm down for you. I want you to be my woman, and I'm ready to handle that nigga Pooh for you tonight if it means you will love me, too.”

“Macho, baby, wait.” She held his face in her hands. “I love you, too! I wanna be with you.”

"Yeah, baby, honestly!" He was geeked up. He stood and pulled her along with him.

"Yes, baby. I love you, and I wanna be with you wholeheartedly."

He picked her up and turned her around in a circle. She laughed, happily. He placed her on her feet and tongued her like he had never tongued her before. They sucked all over each other's lips grinding into one another until LaShawn broke them apart.

"Come on let's get out of here." She pulled him by the hand in a hurry.

Chapter 9

LaShawn was devastated as she stood naked in the full-length mirror. She punched her fist into the palm of her right hand. "Out of all nights, why do you have to come down tonight? Damn you." She was angry at her period for choosing a night that was supposed to be so special for both her and Macho.

Macho knocked on the door to the Hampton Inn's bathroom. "Yo', Goddess, what's going on in there? You ain't jump out the window, did you?" He placed his ear to the door to see if he could hear her.

LaShawn opened it with a solemn look on her face. "Don't be mad at me, but my period just fell. I'm devastated because I swear, I want some of you just as bad as you want some of me." She sighed and held the door frame while looking down at the floor, she slowly trailed her eyes up to his. "Are you angry?"

Macho felt like he was sicker than a person that had caught the Coronavirus. But he couldn't wear his disappointment on his sleeve, he cared about LaShawn too much for that. "Yo', it's all good, baby. Come here." He opened his arms for her.

LaShawn walked into them with her head down. She hugged him. "I know it always seems like it's something with me, but I swear I really like you Macho. I always have, and I wanna be with you in that way because I feel like we deserve each other already."

"Ssshhh, baby, it's all good." He stepped in front of her so that his forehead was to hers, and his lips were brushing over hers as well. Everything happens for a reason. You hear me?"

She nodded. "Yes."

"Now for me, it's about more than what you got between your legs. I know that pussy fye. I know it, I can tell by how you walk, girl." She kissed her lips.

“Shut up.” She playfully slapped his shoulder.

“But I'm serious it’s about more than that for me. Now I still wanna appreciate this body tonight, though. I wanna travel all over your continent and explore your treasures. I ain't gotta part your Red Sea.”

She snickered and shook her head. “You're sure, baby?”

“Hell yeah, I am.” He pulled her to him and kissed her lips gingerly. When a man loves a woman, he'll do anything for her, and sex becomes the last thing, never the first. That's how you know when it’s real, and what I feel for you is real, LaShawn.”

“LaShawn rubbed all over his chest with her little hands while she looked into his eyes longing for him. She didn't know if it was her cycle that had come down that had her so wet, or if it was simply him. Either way she wanted Macho in the worst way imaginable.

Macho led her backward to the bed, and slowly laid her back on it. He straddled her and picked her up until her head was resting just below the headboard. He pulled his black beater off and tossed it to the floor. LaShawn rubbed all over his chocolate abs. He leaned down and kissed her lips.

“You’re a Queen, LaShawn. You are a Goddess, and all I wanna do is worship you like you deserve to be worshipped.” He kissed her lips again and licked all over them before trailing a path with his tongue all the way to her neck. “I love you, baby and I want you so bad.”

LaShawn moaned and arched her back. She was glad she’d been good at counting down the days till her cycle because it afforded her foresight to pack the contents needed in case of an emergency as this was. Macho pulled her shirt over her head and she allowed him to. She released her breasts by unhooking her bra from the front, her titties spilling out of their cups, and into his big hands. "I want you, too, Macho. I promise I do."

Macho leaned forward once again, but this time it was to suck all over her erect nipples that were standing up like gumdrops. He smushed her breasts together and rubbed his face all over them. "You're so perfect, LaShawn. I knew you were, though." He pulled her nipples, then sucked them one by one. He moaned and made loud sucking noises to show her that he was appreciating her gorgeous body.

LaShawn arched her back again and opened her thighs. She remembered it was that time of the month and closed them as close as she could. "I love you, baby." She gasped.

"I love you, too." Macho was already sinking lower.

He got to her stomach and she held her breath. He smiled. His tongue licked all over her abdomen. He could feel the few stretch marks and he appreciated them. LaShawn was a real woman, and those stretch marks mean that she had created life. He admired that, and he loved Lashonda just as much as he did her mother.

He kissed all over her stomach and rubbed her breasts at the same time feeling the hard nipples sticking up against his fingers. He sank lower and pulled her skirt upward. He could smell her scent and it captivated him. It was LaShawn, a woman who he felt deep within his heart that she was supposed to be his Queen.

LaShawn became nervous. "Come on back up here, baby."

Macho kissed and licked along the length of her thighs. He held them open and sucked on her skin. He kissed all the way down to her knee, then licked downward toward her middle. He looked up at her, her eyes were closed. He kissed her along the waistline, and down her other thigh, stopped and continued to squeeze and massage her breasts.

"I want you so bad, LaShawn." He slid up her body and planted himself between her thighs.

LaShawn opened her eyes and stared at him. "I know, baby. I want you, too. It won't be long, I promise it won't."

Macho sucked her neck. "I don't care," he whispered.

"What you say, baby?"

Macho pulled her hard nipples again and sucked her bottom lip. "I said I don't care, I need you so bad. I feel like I been wanting you my whole life." He slipped out of the bed and grabbed her hand. "Come on."

LaShawn felt herself being pulled toward the bathroom. "Where are we going, Macho?"

Macho turned on the shower, adjusted the temperature, and stripped away the remaining articles of his clothing. Once he was naked, pulled off Lashawn's skirt and panties. "I'm finna show you right now what this crazy love shit looks like. I want you, right now. I gotta have you that's all there is to it. Come on." He helped her into the shower stall.

"Macho, I ain't never did nothing like this on my cycle. What if you don't wanna mess with me afterward because our first time was like this? That'll be—"

Macho interrupted her words with his lips. He kissed her passionately and turned her around so that her back was to his chest. The streams of water sprayed all over them. He reached between her thighs and pulled out the string of her tampon. Using basketball skills, he tossed it into the garbage can that was all the way across the room. LaShawn's cycle flowed. The shower water washed its traces away. She felt extremely vulnerable, yet she wanted him worse than ever.

Macho turned her back around. "Do you want me, Goddess, huh?" He was already hard as a rock.

She nodded. "Hell yeah, baby. Right now, please."

Macho pulled her to him and picked her up. He rested her back against the glass shower stall and slid her down on his dick. She engulfed him with her wetness. Her pussy was tight as a fist. They both moaned in unison. Macho kissed her lips, bent his knees and began tossing her up and down deep stroking her pussy, hitting her G spot with each inward thrust.

"Uh! Uh! Uh, Macho! Uh, yes, baby! Yes! Aw, fuck yes!" LaShawn moaned hopping up and down on his pole.

Macho whimpered. It was more than physical for him. He had lusted after LaShawn for so long and now that he was getting his chance to be with her. He became possessive and crazy over her with each thrust. His heart opened and wrapped around LaShawn. She was his woman. He was ready to kill for her. He wanted to make sure she had top of the line everything. There was nothing he wouldn't do for her or anything that he would deny her. He began to stroke her with precision.

LaShawn leaned forward with her mouth wide open, with every plunge of Macho's piece she felt healed. She felt like she was giving herself to a man that appreciated, and really loved her. She needed the connection, she yearned for it. She wrapped her wrists around his neck and screamed as her orgasm rocked her body catching her off guard.

"Awwww shit! Shit, baby!"

Macho felt her walls gripping him over and over. He shuddered. He knew she was cumming. He felt it, and because she was it caused him to do the same. He tossed her up and down faster and faster. He stabbed as hard as he could with his knees bent. He dove deep, hugged her, and smashed her to the wall cumming deep within her channel. He bit into her long neck.

LaShawn trembled and moaned. "I feel you, Macho. I feel you." She kissed all over his lips.

***

An hour later, after both of them had gotten cleaned up, LaShawn scooted backward in the hotel bed and waited for Macho to wrap his arms around her. It didn't take him long. She smiled and got comfortable against his chest. Macho kissed the back of her neck. He snuggled up close to her. She made sure she was as far back on him as she could.

"Yo', LaShawn, I think your body is amazing. I'm letting you know, right now. I'm about to be all over you all the time. If you ain't feeling that you might as well break up with me, right now."

"Aw, so you think that since you got the goods it's cool for me to just break up with you now, huh?" She looked back over her shoulder at him.

"Never that, I ain't never going away from you. What we did just made me even crazier about you." He kissed the back of her neck again. "I need to tell you somethin', though. That way I can let you know in the beginning exactly how I'm about to be over you."

She rolled all the way over until they were facing each other. She held the side of his face with her right hand. "Talk to me, baby. You can tell me anything."

Macho nodded. "Yo', when I was growing up my mother took a lot of beatings from my father until he gave her one too many. He dragged her into the mud, and he treated her like shit for as long as I could remember." He sighed. "From the time I was six-years-old until my mother was killed by my father when I was sixteen-years-old. My mother told me everything that went on inside of her heart. I was her diary. She told me that once I found that woman who made my heart jump, to always go hard for her.

"She told me to kill for her and to make sure I rendered to her nothing but the best—" He paused. "Yo', ever since I first heard your voice, LaShawn, my heart been jumping. From the first time Preston introduced us, I been feeling you. I been thinking about you anytime I was on top of another female. Yo', you got me wide open, and I'm ready to kill for you. That nigga Pooh is on my radar because of you. I don't care what kinda sucka that makes me.

"I'm crazy about you, and I don't want no nigga having access to my woman under no circumstances. I want you to depend on me. I wanna be able to solely depend on you. I love you, and my loyalties are to you first. But you need to know, I am a killa. I do not play in those streets, LaShawn. That murder shit is in me fa real, and I'ma use it to get to the top of the totem pole where we will be able to shine as Royals. This is me, and I am for you." He felt vulnerable having unleashed his inner self.

"Baby, I know who you are. I know what you are about. I'm not an idiot, I know you are a thug and a killa. I'm willing to accept you for who you are because like you I am from the slums of Baltimore as well. I know that shit is real here and that it's kill or be killed. I know we are forced to hustle hard in those streets in order to survive. However, we have to have an end game here, you and me. I see much more for you than the streets, Macho. I wanna help you be your best self. That way we can live and love happily, baby."

"I can't be broke, LaShawn. I was born to be a Boss. I gotta have all the finest things that this world has to offer because I already know in the end where I am going to wind up and it ain't heaven. So, while I'm here I gotta ball hard." He pressed his forehead closer to hers. Their noses touched. They could smell and taste each other's breaths. "I love you with all my heart. All I'm going to ask you to do is to trust me. I promise you ain't gotta worry about no more bills. Fuck that shit. You ain't gotta worry about getting on no punk ass city bus either.

I want you riding foreign, I'll take care of everything. That's how Kings operate."

LaShawn kissed him. "Baby, I don't want you providing for me like I'm incapable. I am an independent woman. I can take care of myself."

"Not no more, I'm your man, I got you. The streets are mine, I'ma own them for you." He flipped her on her back and straddled her. He looked down into her pretty face. "Do you trust me. This is all I need to know. Do you trust me?"

"Yeah, baby, I do. But what about, Preston?"

"We worry about us. I got you, and you got me. That's all that matters." He laid beside her and pulled her to his chest holding her protectively. "Sooner or later we gon' have to let him know what's good but for, right now it's about us. We got a lot of work to do. But we gon' be okay. We gon' start by getting you a whip and moving you out of Guilford. I gotta see my baby in a whole house in the suburbs, so the grind is real. But we got this, bet that."

It all sounded so good to LaShawn that she didn't know what else to say other than, "I love you, Macho!"

Macho kissed her juicy lips. "And I love you, too. We got this."

Chapter 10

It was three weeks later, on a breezy Saturday night in early April. Preston took the Desert Eagle from under his seat and stuffed it in the small of his back before he stepped out of the black Dodge Charger. He looked across the hood of the car at Macho. Macho was adjusting both of his guns. Preston could make out the bulletproof vest across his chest and that seemed to worry him a tad.

"Macho, if you saying these ma'fuckas supposed to be your people. Why the hell is you rocking a bulletproof vest, and two pistols like you're about to go to war or something? Nigga you making me nervous."

Macho zipped up his Marc Jacob Windbreaker jacket and snickered. "Yo', I guess I just wanna be on the safe side. A ma'fucka might be a lil' looney up here but suddenly I wanna live longer. I got a reason too now." He smiled and thought about LaShawn. They'd gotten closer and closer over the past three weeks, and she now captivated his every thought.

Preston gave him a suspicious look. "Nigga, when are you going to introduce me to this new girl? Shorty got you doing shit I have never seen before. I ain't never seen yo' ass smile so much in one day. Word up."

"Yeah, well, nigga get used to it because I feel good. That killa shit is still in me so don't get it twisted." It began to drizzle from the sky. He looked up and a few raindrops dripped right into his eyes.

"We'll talk about that shit later. Can you please tell me what the fuck we're doing all the way in Milwaukee, Wisconsin? How did you link up with your people out here again?" Preston popped his hoodie over his head and zipped his coat as Macho had done. He felt his bulletproof vest itching his chest.

Macho texted his connect and held one finger up to Preston. When he finished, he wiped his phone off from the rain. "I told you these are my blood. They got a stupid plug South of the border, and we need to fuck with them. All I need you to do is to trust me. I'm about to get us rich." He chirped the alarm to his whip and led the way up to the door of the Strip Club.

The parking lot only had a few cars inside it because the club was under construction and set to be moved from the old location to the new one that they were currently going into. Preston looked all around them to see if he spotted any potential threats when he did not, he followed behind Macho and stopped outside of the big, red metal door that led into the back of the strip club.

"Dawg, I don't even know where the fuck Milwaukee is. That's what makes this so crazy."

"That and besides prison, you ain't never stepped outside of Baltimore, nigga." Macho laughed. "Shid, me either, though. This is new for both of us, but it's necessary." He beat on the back door and took a step back. "My people got it together, though. Anytime ma'fuckas don't want you to hit them with no cash upfront you already know they got to be holding."

"Word up." Preston held the handle of his gun and searched the parking lot with his eyes as the rain fell more heavily from the sky. The water popped all over the concrete like pop rocks. Thunder roared overhead after lightning made its presence known.

A minute later the door swung inward, and Montana stood there in front of them. She was dark-skinned, with a voluptuous figure. She had brown eyes and was shorter than both of them. She mugged Preston for a split second. Her eyes became softer when she locked them on Macho. “What's up, cuz? It’s about time yo’ ass made it here.” She waved them inside.

As soon as Macho stepped through the threshold, he hugged her and kissed her cheeks. She smelled like Chanel No.5. “Yo’, traffic was crazy as hell all the way here. You know I don't do the flying thing.”

“Shid, after what happened to Kobe, I be having a hard time being up in that air now, too. That's so sad.” She shook her head at the sudden loss of the Superstar, then looked up and nodded at Preston. “Who is this?”

“This is my brother, Preston. We did a bid in the Feds together. We held each other down with those knives and shit, and ever since we got out we been jammed tight. Dis the only ma’fucka I rotate with. He solid and stump down. Preston, this is Montana.”

“Peace and blessings, Goddess.” Preston held out his hand for her to shake.

Montana frowned at him. “Boy, my cousin said you are family. You better give me a hug.” She held her arms open and walked over to him.

Preston hugged her and smiled. “That's my brother over there, and I'll kill for him.”

“That's all I need to hear. Y'all come on upstairs.” She had two armed female bodyguards that walked closely behind her with their pistols out. They had already been given the word that if anything looked out of line or suspicious, they were to shoot first and ask questions later.

“Yo’, who is Shorty nem that's rocking with you like this? I ain't never seen no hoes strapped and on security before like dem.” Macho kept looking over his shoulder at the bodyguards as they followed close behind them.

“Don't worry about who they is. Just know my bitches are trained to kill and to hate dick. So, their focus is on me and only me. Makaroni been talking about you for two days straight. I know he can't wait to see you." Montana was giddy.

"Who is, Makaroni, Blood?"

"That's her twin and my other cousin. He fucks wit' me, too. When I was in the Feds, he sent me a few thousand that kept me straight until we touched down. He got me a lawyer and all types of shit. He's a good dude." Macho respected Makaroni without a doubt.

"N'all get that shit right. I sent you the five gees, and Mack got you the attorney. Everything we do we split that shit down the middle so let's be mindful of that. Give a Queen her credit when it's due." They came to the second-floor landing of the club and stopped.

From this vantage point, you could overlook the four stages and the huge mainstage along with the two bars. Women on security roamed around downstairs with guns in their hands that had beams on them. They looked up at them ready for action if it called for it.

"I appreciate you, big cuz, I didn't know. Word up, you got my undying loyalty forever, though." Macho hugged Montana again.

She smiled and patted his back. "It's good, now let's go in here and get an understanding."

***

Makaroni was dark-skinned with brown eyes, and a stocky frame. He had a low hair-cut, and a wide nose. He sat at the end of the boardroom table with his fingers clasped together. He looked over both Macho and Preston, before he spoke, "Lil' cuz the hit I'm about to bless you with is not only going to make you filthy rich, but it's going to give you more power than you may know what to do with. It's that serious." He stood up and rested his hands on the table. "Now on the flip side, it's going to have you beefing with some serious ass people that belong to Cartels, Mafias, and even the government. When you reach a certain status money wise that's when you find out who you really have to answer to and war against. It's levels to this shit fa real.

"Right now, don't nobody that's anybody really know who you lil' niggas are, but when I bless you with this life-changing Heroin all that shit is about to change and the both of you will officially become targets on another level. Don't get me wrong them small niggas gon' wanna fuck wit' you, too, but they can be easily crushed. You'll find that out, too. I guess my only question to the both of you before we move any further, is if you are ready to put your life, and the lives of your family in danger every second of every day in order to live above standard?"

Montana came and sat on the arm of his chair.

Macho powered his head and thought about LaShawn and Lashonda. He imagined somebody hurting them on the strength of his hustle or the size of the bag that he had put up in a safe. It made him angry and worried at the same time. He knew he would die before he allowed anything to happen to either one of them. He was crazy about LaShawn and he was getting there with Lashonda as well.

Preston thought about his sister, LaShawn, his niece Lashonda, and his mother Ilene. It would crush his heart if anything was to happen to either of them because somebody was trying to hurt him. "Yo', I don't understand how us being in the streets the way that we are right now doesn't put our people at risk the same way? But even with you telling me this, and I can only speak for myself. I'm ready to get my bread up because there's a lot of changes I wanna make around my hood, and for my family as well. It's fucked up that we gotta reach into the dope game to make shit happen, but it is what is it. I'm hungry and this my nigga. I'm riding wit' him until the wheels fall off."

Macho nodded. "Yeah, big cuz, we're animals. We know how to protect our homes. I mean, we been doing a good job this far. Whatever you are about to bless us with will only help us beef up our security personnel, and I'm most definitely with that. So, what's really good?"

Montana hopped off the arm of Makaroni's chair and clapped her hand together. The boardroom's door opened and in came a light-skinned female with green eyes and a gorgeous figure. She wore black from head to toe. Black pants, a black top, and a black half-mask that covered fifty percent of her face. She handed Montana a briefcase and walked out of the room with her ass jiggling. She closed the door.

Montana took the briefcase and set it on the table. She did the combination and popped the locks. She looked into Macho's eyes. "Lil' cuz the only reason we are blessing you with this is because you are a Stevens, and you have a right to this work because of your bloodline. Our family has invested blood, and pain to keep this drug running through our familial veins. Because of your bloodline, you are destined to be rich, and so I present to you the Rebirth." She reached inside the briefcase and pulled out a sheet of aluminum foil. She took a small spoon and dumped a portion of the drug on to it. It was tan and full of crystals.

Makaroni stood up. "Under no circumstances will you ever inject or snort this drug. Under no circumstances will you allow anybody that works under you to use this drug. This drug is highly addictive, and it will ruin a person's life at the first try of it. Nobody is strong enough to overcome its effects. It's specifically designed in our labs to make sure of that. Once you release this dope on the Maryland streets you will be swarmed, and your real dope boy lives will begin. In a matter of months, if you are doing what you are supposed to, you will emerge as drug lords."

"But on the other hand, if you aren't you will be slain quickly by the many predators that are waiting for you to step into the Shark-infested waters." Montana looked into Macho's eyes. "I know all this shit seems so far-fetched but I'm telling you that it's all serious, and the truth."

Preston didn't think that they were overexaggerating at all. In fact, he felt like they might have been minimizing what becoming prominent drug lords in the game meant. He'd done a lot of research while he was in Federal prison about Mafia members, the Cartel, and Drug Lords South of the border and what he found out was that the more money they made the more problems they wound up having, and it appeared that everybody became their enemy, even those that started out close to them.

They needed to take the game serious, and he most definitely intended on doing just that.

Macho stood up. "Y'all say that hustling this shit is in my bloodline anyway, right?"

Montana nodded her head. "It sure is."

"Well, then it's already in me to know what to do. I ain't gon' fuck off my inheritance to the streets. If it's time for a mafucka to level up then that's what I'ma do. Me and my nigga. Just show us how this shit works, and we gon' go from there."

Makaroni stepped beside him and rested his hand on his back. "We gon' be with you every step of the way because it's in our best interest that you shine hard. As long as you are, we will be as well. But y'all strap up because it's a lot of stuff that you need to know."

"Yeah, we're about to teach you how to take over the Game in a matter of months," Montana added, sliding her arm around Makaroni's waist.

Preston stood up and clapped his hands together loudly. "Well, let's get this show on the road!"

Chapter 11

A month after Preston and Macho got back from Milwaukee, Wisconsin connecting with Makaroni and Montana they had made major footing within the slums of Baltimore. Macho took his portions of the Rebirth and pumped it into the Dunman Way Apartments. The Dunman Way apartments were silver brick townhomes located in the heart of the ghetto of Baltimore. The area was drug-infested, and home to some of the deadliest savages. Macho was born and raised in Dunman Way. He felt like the hood belonged to him, and he was ready to crush anybody that told him it didn't.

A month after they returned from Wisconsin, he was up to a hundred thousand dollars in the safe, and fifty thousand invested in the streets for the purchase of guns, food, and drugs for his crew of savages, along with their transportation. He made sure that any Cutthroat killa that ran under him stayed with a handgun, and an assault rifle close by their person. He assigned them in pairs. Each person was assigned to watch out for their pair mate as well as the rest of the family in the crew. Each person was to hold the other accountable for foul behavior, slacking, drug usage, or anything that would work against the family. In exchange for their cooperation, Macho made sure his savages were well taken care of, and that their families never had to worry about bills or protection.

In the sixth week after he and Preston's return, Macho thought it would be cool for him and his savages to throw a block party for the citizens on Dunman Road. Dunman Road is where the Dunman Way apartments were located. So, they shut down four blocks of Dunman Road, and Macho put his killas on patrol as security to make sure nothing got out of hand with the people in the community or those within his crew.

Lashonda was away visiting Pooh's parents in South Philly, but LaShawn stayed behind and thought it would be cool to spend some time with her man enjoying the block party. Macho pulled up in front of LaShawn's apartment complex in his new black on black Dodge Durango. He held the passenger's door open for her to jump inside. When she was secured away, he jogged around to the other side with the sunlight reflecting off the chains that were around his neck. He opened the driver's door and got inside of it. There was a security follow car behind them with three people, a driver and two shooters. Macho wanted to make sure that whenever LaShawn rolled with him she was as safe as could be.

He pulled away from the curb. "You already know we are about to have to spend the hell out of your brother. He's already over here, and his goons are on high alert. But I missed you though, Baby."

LaShawn smiled. "Right, can you please tell me that before you get to telling me anything else about what Preston is doing?" She rolled her eyes. "Then we got a car following us watching our every move so we can't even kiss the way I need to feel you. Damn, man, I'm so lost because I need my man and it seems like it's a million restrictions keeping me away from you."

"What, you got me twisted. Those rolling behind me ride with me. They are loyal to me first. You better bring yo' lil' sexy ass across this console and give me my kiss." He brought the truck to a halt at a stop sign.

LaShawn was giddy as she unleashed her seat belt and came into his arms. She hugged his body and kissed his lips hungrily. She hadn't had the proper time to spend with him in two days, and to her, it felt like an eternity. Her tongue danced with his, she ended kissing his lips and rubbing his face. "Mmm." She took her seat again.

"You feel better, Baby? I know I do."

"I was finna say because you ain't seen me in the same amount of time that I ain't seen you. I bet not be the only one crazy in this relationship." She said seriously.

Macho looked over at her with a sly smile on his face. "Never that, I love the fuck out of you, you already know that. I'm just a little bit more subtle with everything. But you already know that I'm crazy."

"Well, subtle ain't what got me to cross over to you so I'ma need you to be less subtle, and more like that hungry animal that's pouring his heart out to me to get me to cross over and be with you. Those were the days that kept me fiening for you just as hard as you were for me. You're the first man that had me up all night thinking about you, and missing you like crazy. I been going nuts these last few days without my doses of Macho," she grunted. "You got anything you wanna share with me?" She batted her eyelashes.

Macho snickered. "Yeah, I missed you, Baby. I been going crazy without you, too. You're the love of my life, and I'm sorry for going so hard in these streets. I been out here getting things together for us, though. But it still doesn't make up for the time I spent away from my Jewel. But I do love you, and my absence ain't been in vain. Here, I want you to put this in the safe that I bought you." He pulled a roll of hundreds out of the console totaling ten thousand dollars.

LaShawn took it. "Damn, Macho, how much is this?" She thumbed through a few of the bills and saw that they were all hundreds. Her eyes got as big as saucers.

"It's ten more thousand. If you ain't spent shit you should have fifty in all. I already told you, I don't want you paying no bills, I got that. Now that is ten right there, and this is another gee just for your pocket or in case Lashonda wants or needs anything. Cool?"

LaShawn was finding it so hard to keep it together. But it seemed that lately every time she was in Macho's presence, he found a way to make her emotional. The things he did for her no other man ever had. Macho was focused on her long-term stability, and he acted as if he didn't want anything in return other than her love. This made LaShawn feel weak. “Baby, first off, thank you for the money. Secondly, I don't like to keep accepting it because I don't have anything to give you in exchange for it, right now. It makes me feel like a gold digger and I am so far from that.”

“You're giving me you, and your time is precious. But you, are the most precious. Yo’, I love you and this is how it looks when a man that's out here getting it, is in love with a woman. You ain't doing nothing wrong, and neither am I.” He glanced at her and kept rolling. “As far as your gold digger comment goes. Baby, once a woman has a child and is cursed with a bum ass baby daddy like that nigga, Pooh, she is forced to do whatever it takes to survive. The title of gold-digging no longer applies to her, it’s called surviving. The reason why I hit your hand the way that I do is because I wanna see you shine bright. I wanna make sure that you and LaShawn have financially secure futures. My next breath is never promised, but y'alls are, well at least more than mine anyway.” He laughed. “Bottom line your good, Boo. This is us, and we got each other, right?” He raised his right eyebrow.

“Right,” LaShawn whispered. She was still feeling a way because she was so used to being independent. Now she felt more like a dependent.

Macho looked over at her. “We going to roll through the strip a few times, then you and I are going to have a nice dinner where we will get to know each other a lot better. How does that sound to you?”

LaShawn smiled. “As long as we are spending time together then it’s all good with me. I love you so much, Macho, please know that.”

Macho stared at her for a moment and nodded. “Boo I do know, and I love you, too.”

***

Pooh threw his hoody over his head and jogged to the black Chevy Astro van that was filled with five of his Payroll killas. He sat in the backseat and was handed a hundred shot Draco from Lil’ Tike who was a seventeen-year-old shooter and had been ever since he was twelve. Tike had a blue bandana around his face and an AK47 over his lap. He nodded at Pooh.

“Say, Cuz, we just strolled around the strip and them Cutthroat niggas out there partying like they ain't got a care in the world. I say we wet they ass and let them know that this shit is real. We wit’ you, Pooh.”

Pooh looked behind him and nodded his head at the killas. He pulled his bandana over his face and frowned. “Nigga we hit anybody and everybody. We aim for them red niggas but if somebody else gets in the way that ain't our fault. Buss these guns until them bitches go empty, it’s as simple as that,” he ordered.

Tike slammed the magazine harder into his Kay and cocked it on the side. “No mercy, nigga. We finna see how much these blood niggas really like to bleed. Word up.”

Pooh laughed at that. “Yo’ Chauncey, come through the back way. We’ll catch they ass off guard on Colgate Avenue.”

“I'm already two steps ahead, Boss. We'll be there in fifteen minutes, be ready.”

***

Preston rolled down the strip with Kayley in the passenger's seat of his black on black Dodge Magnum. She rested her hand on his thigh and squeezed it. This was their second time cruising around the block just taking in the scenery. He had the *Summer Walker 'Over It'* album crooning out of the speakers, and a slight smile on his face. Everywhere he looked his people were having fun. They were eating big plates of food. They were banging their head to the multiple big speakers that were set up along the blocks.

Kids ran back and forth chasing one another, while others jumped rope, or played basketball in the middle of the street. He even saw that the dope addicts were laughing and eating big plates of food that he and Macho provided. They had paid off the city cops for six hours in order to have the block party, and for him, it felt good to not have the local authorities rolling around all day. His men could handle the hood's security, he didn't need nothing that was blue.

"I really think this is amazing, Preston. This is the type of stuff that you see back home in Houston. I admire you for giving back like this." She squeezed his thigh harder and rubbed it.

"These are my people. If we don't take care of them, who will? My goal is to buy the Dunman apartments from the city and reprice the rent for all these folks. I want the apartments to be affordable, or for low-income mothers to live in. I was talking to one lady and she was saying that her rent done went up twice this year already. It seems like the city is trying to push these people out or something. I ain't trying to hear that shit. If they push us out where will we go?"

"You're straight. You'll have somewhere to go but they won't. The whole gentrification is real. Whenever the government or the city wants to move our people around it's like we don't have any other choice other than to move. We've been getting bullied since the beginning of time and it sucks."

"Yeah, well, not no more. That's why it's imperative that we run up a check and get the biggest bag possible. You can't do shit when you're broke. The only thing the world responds to is money, that's just the way it is. So, I'm forced to get it. When I get enough of it, I'm going to change some lives, including my own. You can bet that."

Kayley nodded. "That's what's up. I hope you don't go changing too much, though. Especially not the way you feel about me." She glanced at him from the corners of her eyes. "I saw how a bunch of these females in this hood was peeping you when we were walking up and down the strip. I am a very humble female, but I'll bring this Texas shit out of me quick over my man. Don't get one of these hoes fucked up, Preston, straight up."

"Whoa, whoa, whoa, Baby, where did all of that come from? I ain't thinking about nobody but you. Damn, I thought we was on our black love shit?"

"We are, but I know women and I see that you are wanted in this hood. Everybody looking for a savior, and I get it, but I ain't going. Fuck that."

"You ain't never gotta worry about me disrespecting you like. I'm man enough to come and tell you if I feel like fuckin' off. That shit ain't even on my mental. I'm too financially focused on the game to slip up like that, and besides, you are enough for me. It's too many mafuckin' diseases out here for all of that."

"Yeah, I know. But I guess I just say that to say that—" She stopped and bucked her eyes. It took her a second to understand what she was looking at, then the shots started firing.

***

Pooh waited until Preston's Magnum began to roll past Colgate Avenue before his driver stepped on the gas to block them off. Pooh threw open the side door and set on the edge of the van's floor before he began to shoot his Draco with the intent to kill everybody inside of Preston's whip.

Boom! *Boom*! *Boom*! *Boom*!

The bullets caught Preston off guard. His side window shattered. He felt two bullets slam into his shoulder. He swerved and crashed his car into a parked car that was in the middle of Colgate Avenue. His shoulder throbbed like crazy. The bullets continued to chop at his whip. He undid his seat-belt, pulled Kayley to the floor and jumped on top of her to shield her from the bullets. Pooh and his team parked their van in the front of Preston's whip, they hopped out of the van and lit up Preston's Magnum with round after round of ammunition. When they finished, they hopped back into the van and scurted away from the scene with smoke billowing from their tires.

Chapter 12

It had been a week since Preston had been shot two times by Pooh and his crew. Kayley hadn't heard from her man and he hadn't been on Facebook or any of his social media accounts and this worried her. She kept having flashbacks about the night when they'd been under attack. She was sure that if Preston hadn't pulled her to the floor of the car and jumped on top of her that she would've been killed. When Pooh's van finally rolled away, and she had the chance to step outside of the car she saw that her passenger's door had been filled with holes. Many of the bullets struck the passenger's seat right where she'd been sitting. So not only had Preston saved her life once, but twice. She felt like she owed him.

It was a Wednesday night and she'd been pacing back and forth inside of her apartment worrying about Preston when her doorbell rang catching her off guard. She jumped from the sheer shock of the noise. Her heart was already pounding in her chest making it hard for her to breathe. The shooting was still fresh and heavy on her brain.

She stepped to the intercom and held the button. "Who's down there?"

"It's Marco girl, buzz me up."

Kayley found this odd. She hadn't spoken to Marco in a few weeks and it wasn't like him to pop up out of the blue without texting or Facebooking her first. She buzzed the door open for him and hurried to throw on a pair of pants since she was walking around in just a comfortable pair of panties. Before she could button them all the way Marco was knocking at her door. She casually walked to it, and unlocked it, pulling it open.

Marco strolled inside and stopped in front of her. He held his arms open for her. "What's good, Mami?"

Kayley closed the door and locked it. She stepped into Marco's arms and hugged him back. "Nothing, I was just pacing trying to get my mind together. What brings you here tonight? You smell like alcohol."

Marco was tipsy. "I been drinking a lil' Patron but it's all good. I ain't seen you in a while. I been worried about you. What's up with you?" He followed her into the kitchen.

Kayley opened the refrigerator and grabbed two bottled waters. She handed Marco one and took the other one walking past him. "I been going through some thangs, but I'm good, though. You telling me you came all the way over here just to ask me that?"

Marco laughed and set the bottled water on the table. "N'all, there's been a few other things that came to my attention but I wanna do this a little bit at a time. I need to ask you something and I want you to tell me the truth. If you lie to me there's going to be consequences. Do you understand that?"

Kayley had been drinking from her bottled water she spilled some of it on her blouse upon hearing his last statement. "What are you talking about consequences?"

Marco took the bottled water from her hand and set it on the table. "Yo', I heard you fucking with a black dude. That's the first question."

"That's not a question, Marco, that's a statement. And whose business is it but mine if I am?" She glared at him.

"It's mine. You already know who I had in mind for you before you got here from Houston. You're supposed to be fuckin' with, Roberto. His family is connected and he's the only one of the crew that is fawning all over your black ass. We have to take advantage of that."

"Excuse you." She mugged him with her nose flared.

"You know what I mean, and I don't mean it like that."

"Well, it's exactly how you said it. But for the record, I don't like Roberto. I am black, yes, my man is as well, and it's a shame I even have to explain myself to you. I am twenty years old. I'm a grown-ass woman, you don't own me." She brushed past him and walked into her living room.

"Okay, well, that brings me to my next question. Are you fuckin' with one of the black dudes that I now know ripped me off?"

Kayley's heart skipped a beat. "I don't know what you are talking about," she lied. "I thought you didn't know who ripped you off. You said that over and over. Now all of a sudden you know?" she scoffed.

"Kayley this ain't a fuckin' game and I ain't stupid. I heard about how Macho and that Preston nigga that you're fucking with is over in Dundalk balling out of control with the product that they stole from me. I also know that you knew they hit me. It's beginning to feel like you had something to do with it. Now convince me that I'm wrong." He slipped behind her and took a hold of her waist.

Kayley spun out of his embrace and faced him. "I don't know what you're talking about, Marco. You sound like you're doing a whole lot of fishing, and ain't nobody got time for that. In fact, I'm kind of tired. We need to discuss this shit at another time." She walked to the front door and unlocked it.

Marco walked further into her apartment. "Ever since you got to Baltimore, I been keeping you straight. I've treated you as nothing less than my sister. Made sure that you stayed fly, and hit your pockets because we are technically family, but now I find out you are sleeping with one of the enemies and that shit got me vexed."

"It's time to go, Marco, because you are bugging. I don't know what the fuck you are talking about, but you sound like you done lost your mind. So, bye." Kayley needed to find a way to get in touch with Preston to let him know that Marco was on to him. She worried about his safety, and she wondered why he wasn't answering to her reaching out to him?

"Alright, it's cool. I'ma leave your house but I just wanna let you know that it's fucked up how you played me. I was supposed to be your brother. Who gives a fuck if it's only by marriage? Family is family, but it's all good." He stepped to the door beside her and took a hold of the knob.

"Why are you just looking at me like that? You can leave." She tried to open the door.

Marco blocked her path and locked it back. Before she could gather her thoughts, he picked her up and fell to the floor with her. Kayley punched at his face and hit at his head. Marco took the assault in stride. He ripped open her blouse like a brute and tore off her bra. Her chocolate breasts came spilling out to his view.

"Get off me, Marco! What the fuck is wrong with you?" She kept fighting at him.

"You think shit sweet. You think your nigga can rip me off and ain't nobody gon' pay for it? You got me fucked up." He unbuttoned her pants and scooted backward pulling them off. When he got them off her ankles, he threw them across the room and got between her thighs again. His hand rubbed over the crotch of her panties.

Kayley kicked at him connecting with his chest. He let out a whoosh of air. He took her right ankle and brought his elbow down on it at full speed spraining it. "Owww!" she screamed.

"Ever since you got over here, I been wanting to fuck this pussy. You wanna give it out to a bunch of backstabbers, well you gon' give me some of it too, then. He ripped her panties to shreds. Got between her thighs and unzipped his pants. He was already hard as a rock. He searched for her opening while she swung and scratched at him. His head found her opening, he slammed it home and plunged for six hard strokes. He groaned and came before he could even get started.

Kayley sat up and punched him in the nose as hard as she could, busting it. Blood squirted across his cheeks. She brought her head forward and head-butted him as hard as she could. This knocked him off her. He groaned in pain. His nose was broken. She jumped up and ran into the kitchen to grab the biggest knife she could find. She wrapped her hand around the butcher's knife and rushed back into the living room. Marco was just getting up. Kayley was out of her mind. He'd just violated her in a way that she could never forgive him for. She bull-rushed him at full speed and slammed the knife as hard as she could into his chest.

Marco felt the blade of the knife pierce his skin and break through his ribs. The sharp point landed into his heart and burst the organ. Blood spurt all over his internal system. He took a deep breath and blood poured out of his mouth. He fell backward.

Kayley stood over him with her knife dripping blood. Her chest heaved up and down. She felt like she had ice in her throat. Her eyes were bucked wide open. “I hate you, Marco, you coward! What type of man rapes a woman? I hate you!”

Marco tried to get up, but he was bleeding profusely internally. Blood poured out of his nose and mouth. He fell back to the floor coughing up more blood. He closed his eyes. His body began to shake and turn cold. He wanted to cry out for help, but it was of no use. He opened his eyes one final time. His last sights were of Kayley standing over him with the big butcher's knife in her hand.

***

The next morning it was bright, sunny, and scorching hot with intense humidity, Kayley was up and parked outside of the Baltimore district one county jail when Preston came out of it holding a clear plastic bag with a few items he'd been arrested with inside it. After being shot twice his probation officer placed him on a hold while they investigated his case. He hated the system. He didn't understand how he being the victim coulda been arrested for somebody shooting him, but he took it and keep it moving.

Kayley got out of the car and ran to him at full speed. When she made it to him and jumped, he caught her in his arms. She broke into tears. "Why would you do me like that, Preston, huh? Why? I didn't know where you were, or if you were even alive."

"Baby, I didn't do it on purpose. These people had me locked down, and they monitored everything that I did. They only allowed me to call out to my immediate family for twenty minutes once a week, and I didn't have your address. LaShawn don't know you, so I was stuck. I been going crazy missing you, too." He kissed all over her face and set her down. "Luckily, you hit her up on Facebook and she got right back to you." He put her down and brushed her hair out of her face.

The sunlight shined off her dark skin, she was super fine to him. "Baby I killed, Macro. I kilt him." She felt hysterical.

"What?" Preston looked around, he placed his arm around her neck and walked her to her car. He opened the driver's door and helped her to sit inside of it. Once she was in, he jogged around to the other side and pulled on the handle. She popped the lock, he got in.

Kayley covered her face with her hands and broke down. "His father been hitting me up asking me if I've seen or heard from Marco. I lied and said I didn't. My mother has, too. I don't know what to do. I can't believe I killed him." She started to cry.

Preston rubbed her back, he was in shock. "Why did you do it, Baby?"

"He raped me, Preston. He put his little fucking piece inside of me. I was so disgusted that I killed him, and I shouldn't have." She broke down thinking about her impending consequences.

"Where is he now?"

"His body is in my tub inside of my apartment. I didn't know what else to do with him."

"Alright, well first off, I'm glad that you are okay. Secondly, fuck that nigga. If you wouldn't have killed him I would have so you just beat me to it. Thirdly, I got you, ain't nobody gon' ever find out about this. Preston, gon' take care of it. Come on, let's go."

***

That night ley helped Preston burn Marco's body in a metal garbage can next to the train tracks off Wilshire Street. Then Preston placed Marco's remains in a series of plastic bags where he beat his bones for two hours straight with a sledgehammer until his bones were dust. They took the bones and the rest of his carnage and poured it into the huge river, then set fire to the plastic bags. Preston kept his arm around Kayley protectively while they watched the remnants of Marco float away. He turned her around to face him.

"Baby forget about this. As hard as I know it's going to be to do it, you have to. We gotta act like this night never happened. Just know that I love you, and I got you. We are in this together. Ride and die. You feel me?"

Kayley nodded. "For life, Preston. That's on my soul."

Chapter 13

"Dawg after all that stuff that happened with Kobe I can't believe I'm actually sitting on a damn helicopter with you. I ain't gon' even lie I'm scared as a muthafucka," Preston admitted feeling his teeth chattering together.

He didn't like heights, never had, and after his second favorite basketball player Kobe Bryant and his daughter was killed in one amongst a group of other people, he was extremely reluctant. But Macho had convinced him that the flying was necessary if they were trying to expand their operations and connect with East coasters beyond Baltimore. So, Preston gave in, but he was starting to regret it because his nerves wouldn't calm down even for a second.

"That was back in January, and you can't allow one tragedy to keep you bound for your whole life. Besides, it's already written how you're going to die and when, so you can't cheat death. It's gon' happen when it's supposed to. Now nigga break up out of that scary shit because you are missing some incredible views of the East coast." Macho adjusted the headphones on his head and looked out of the big windows.

Preston felt like he needed to use the bathroom. His stomach was flipping over and over. He'd passed gas twice and still didn't feel like he was getting any relief. To him, the helicopter felt like it was seconds away from going down. He didn't see how anybody could fly on one every single day. He was losing his mind. "Yo', Macho, Kid I'm about to be sick."

"What?" Macho looked over at Preston and saw that his face was sheer white. "What the fuck?" He grabbed his homie and held his face in both of his hands. "Dawg what's up with you. Are you tripping out about this flying shit like that?"

Preston was shivering. "I can't do this, Macho. Yo', I ain't built to be flying in nobody's sky. We gotta take this bitch down like asap." He started shivering so bad that he was borderline about to have a seizure.

"Okay, dawg, yo' just chill. Say man how far are we away from New York?" he hollered this to the pilot.

"About an hour. Everything okay back there?" The Jewish pilot turned around and saw how Macho was attending to Preston.

"Say man turn yo' ass around and focus on all those controls and shit. We got this back here," Preston ordered pointing toward the front of the Chopper.

"Yes, Sir." The pilot turned around and got back to work.

"Look, Preston, why don't you close your eyes, bruh? We got an hour left. All you gotta do is close your eyes and try your best to drift off. If you want too, we can spark a fat ass blunt of that OG Kush and get gassed up. What you wanna do?"

Preston shook his head. "Nall fuck that, I'm high enough. That mighta been my mistake because had I not smoked, I wouldn't be so ma'fuckin' paranoid about this bitch going down, right now. Fuck!" He slammed his fist into the seat and closed his eyes.

"Yo', calm down, Kid." Macho looked him over. "Blood if this bitch go down then we'll die on this ma'fucka together, word up. If you go, I wanna go, too."

Preston opened his eyes and frowned at Macho. "You my nigga to the death dawg. Fuck."

"You already know that. We got less than an hour. We can rollback, but for now, let's do this shit together. A'ight."

"Cool, fuck it! Yo', why don't you tell me about this lil' female you got ducked off? When are you going to let me meet her?" Preston closed his eyes back as the helicopter shook just a tad.

Macho laughed. "When the time is right. Shorty is one of those in the air type of girls so if you wanna meet her you are gonna have to catch her in the clouds with me. You think you can do that?"

"Hell n'all, I guess I'll meet her ass when I meet her." Preston was dead serious.

Macho busted out laughing. "Yo', what's good with you and Kayley, though? You about to lock that shit down or what?"

"She pregnant, Kid. You already know that deadbeat shit ain't in me at all. I'ma hold her down to the fullest of my potential, I don't know if I'm done one hundred percent with being out in those streets, but I most definitely can't see myself hurting her. I think I'm ready to be a father. I done got a lot of practice with, Lashonda."

"Pregnant, Blood, word? Damn, you put that shit in there for real, that's what's up." He shook up with Preston. "That just means we gotta go extra hard to secure this plug. They wanna cop the Rebirth from us and flood a few boroughs in New York City. We could see every bit of a million a week if we do shit right. If my cousins are willing to send us that much shit every week, which I am sure they will be once we get a fool understanding and I break shit down for them piece by piece. We are talking about some life-altering shit, bruh. I didn't know this shit was going to come into fruition this fast, but it is so we gotta roll with it."

"Yeah." Preston kept his eyes closed. "Yo', where do you be meeting all these people at anyway? It seems like you're always finding a plug on something. That's what's up, though."

"I just don't wanna go back to that broke shit again, Preston. I hated not having no ends in my pocket or being forced to go without just because a ma'fucka didn't have the right cash flow. That shit was whack ass fuck. Now we cop whatever we wanna cop, and we make shit happen for them. That's how it's supposed to be, and that's how it's going to stay. I got big dreams, Kid, like huge ones. This dope game shit ain't hard. It's all about who you know, and how you finesse they ass. The higher we climb the more I'm learning. I'm on my way to the top, bruh. You gon' be right alongside me when I get there."

"I wanna change Baltimore, Kid. I don't wanna do this dope slanging shit forever. I want more than just this living. My moms always told me that I had greatness inside of me, well I believe her. I need to get her to rehab man, and I don't feel like she's going to go unless I build the building myself. So, that's what I wanna do, or I at least wanna be able to put her in a topnotch rehab facility. I love her, Kid. I need her to be around for a long time. In addition to her, I wanna take care of LaShawn and Lashonda, too. I gotta move them out of the hood and make sure they never have to want for anything ever again. I'ma do whatever I have to in order to make that happen."

Macho's face grew slack. "Yo', LaShawn is strong, Kid. I don't think you're finna have to worry about her or Lashonda. They are going to be alright, I'm certain of that."

Preston nodded his head. "Yeah, I guess, but I still gotta do what I have to in order to solidify that they stay straight. If I don't take care of them ain't nobody else gon' do it. Ain't nothing but goofy ass niggas left in the world. I can't expect my sister to catch a good man no more. So, I gotta step up to the plate for her."

Macho felt like Preston was hitting him with a slug. He tensed his muscles. "Yo', if it's one thing I know about LaShawn it's that she's very smart. She'll find a good man, and she'll compliment him. She'll be alright. You need to be focused on Kayley, and y'all new baby that's gonna be here in no time."

Preston opened his eyes in shock. "Damn you're right, I just thought about that shit. I'm about to be a father. Holy shit."

Macho started cracking up. "Nigga that shit just hit you." He busted out laughing while missing LaShawn. He couldn't wait to get back to her.

***

It was four o'clock in the afternoon when Pooh stepped up to LaShawn's door and knocked on it three times. He held a bouquet of roses behind his back. He checked his surroundings. He had two cars full of Hittas watching his every move just in case Preston or Macho decided to make an appearance. He'd heard through the grapevine that LaShawn was messing with Macho. He'd even had them followed on more than one occasion and confirmed that they were actually together because it was reported to him that they were kissing, hugging, and getting along quite romantically.

That pissed him off. Macho's name was ringing in the streets, and he was getting a nice amount of money which made him a threat, and although Pooh didn't want nothing to do with LaShawn he couldn't stand for her to be happy with another man. He'd rather see her broken down and struggling then up and flourishing. He needed to pull out all the stops, and that's what he had planned to do.

LaShawn opened the door to her duplex apartment and frowned at Pooh. "Boy, what are you doing here? You don't get Lashonda for a whole other six days."

Pooh came from behind his back with the bouquet of roses. "Look I been stupid, and I apologize for treating you less than a woman. Every time I see my daughter, I see a small version of you. I love her with all my heart which helped me realize that I love you as well." He checked his right and his left to make sure that he was still in the clear. "Look, LaShawn, can I at least come in to talk to you for a second, please?"

LaShawn felt completely taken off guard. She looked Pooh over like he'd lost his mind. "Pooh, what the hell is going on with you boy? What con are you running?"

"I'm not running no con, LaShawn. I wanna right my wrongs. You are the mother of my child and I think it's important that I get things right with you. Now, can you please give me a chance to hear me out?"

LaShawn searched his face for a long time. All the things that he'd ever done to her flashed through her mind and it made her angry. She wanted to punch him in his face. But then he smiled, and she saw the same dimples on his cheeks as she saw daily on Lashonda's. If she didn't owe it to anybody else, she owed it to her daughter to see what Pooh was talking about.

If it was a con, she was sure she would pick it up right away. "Come on in, Pooh."

Pooh smiled, he turned around and gave his security team the be on point sign, before he stepped into LaShawn's house. "I appreciate you giving me a chance to explain myself, LaShawn. I just been thinking, and I know it's time for me to be a man." He handed the roses out to her again.

LaShawn closed the door. "How long have you known that I've been messing with Macho? And is this the best con game you can come up with? Some funky ass roses! Nigga step yo' trifling ass game up. My man buys me diamonds. Roses are for a week, diamonds are forever."

Pooh was breathless. “Yo’, what are you talking about? I didn't even know that you were fucking with that sucka ass nigga.” He became heated.

LaShawn stepped up to him. “I used to be weak, Pooh, but I ain't no more. You can't run that bullshit ass game on me and think it’s going to lead me to giving you some of my body because it ain't. You are old news. I don't want nothing to do with you, and if Lashonda wasn't in the middle of us. Boy, well let's just say you wouldn't even be a thought for me. Now take your funky ass flowers and get the hell out of my house. I don't want shit to personally do with you. Do we understand each other?”

“Man bitch, I'll—”

Two of Macho's shooters crept out of the hallway with Mach .90s in their hands. Their red beams scanned all over Pooh's face for a kill shot. They slowly moved toward him thirsty for LaShawn to give them the word to shoot him dead. Pooh raised his arms and backed toward the door.

LaShawn stepped in his face. “If you ever think you are going to put your hands on me again without losing your life you got the game all the way fucked up. Nigga, you're only alive because I'm letting you live on the strength of, Lashonda. Don't play with your luck. Now get the fuck out of my house. Now!”

Pooh backed up and nodded his head. He grabbed the door handle and slammed the roses down on the carpet. “Fuck you, LaShawn! That bitch ass nigga ain't gon’ be with you for long. Boss niggas fuck wit’ boss bitches. You a bum! Fuck you!” He stormed out the door and slammed it.

The shooters scurried to the window and kept their beams on the back of his head until he pulled away from her house heated.

***

"So, that's all we're asking. If you can supply us with ten bricks of the Rebirth a month for ninety days straight. We will open up the market in New York for your product, and in the fourth month we can promise you no less than a million a week as long as your product is steady," Angela Simms said sitting at the head of the table with her fingers tapping against each other. She was light-skinned, with brown eyes, and a gorgeous figure that plastic surgery had a major role in enhancing. "Is this possible?"

Macho looked over a text message from his lead security personnel. It read: *Pooh just left LaShawn crib. Everything kosher*. Macho wanted to pick up his phone and inquire further but he knew he had to attend to his business at hand. "Yo', that don't seem like a problem. Let me holler at my people, I'll get back to you in twenty-four hours. But I am sure we can close this deal. I appreciate your making time for us, too. Word up."

Angela Simms smiled. "Well, Macho, you go ahead and talk to your people and let them know that demand is high out here in New York, and the quality supply is very low. The sooner they get back to you will be the sooner we can all get just a whole lot richer." She winked at him.

Macho caught it and ignored it. His mind was on the safety of LaShawn. He stood up. "Well, it was nice meeting you, Ms. Simms. Me and my mans will be in touch with you real soon." He came around the table to shake her hand.

Angela Simms looked up at him and ran her tongue across her teeth. "Perhaps before you leave New York Macho, you and I can have a sit down in private to discuss how I can take you and your organization to the next level?" She smiled at him. "I've got a few paragraphs about how you guys are doing things over in Baltimore and I think I can open a few doors for you just as long as you are willing to, you know, listen to a woman."

"Gender ain't never meant nothing to me when it comes to business. I'll take you up on that offer, but it will have to be another time. Right now, I have more pressing matters back home. I'll be in touch, Preston let's roll."

Angela Simms watched the pair head out of her board-room and nodded her head at their departure. Never in life had she ever been snubbed so bad the way she felt Macho had done her, not only did it bruise her ego, but it left her intrigued. She was a wealthy woman with her hand in all facets of the under-world. Her reach was long and wide. She was able to get any-thing she desired, and now she desired Macho, and she had every intention of getting him.

Chapter 14

Two weeks later, the plug through Montana and Makaroni all the way back to New York was secure. Macho and Preston were making money hand over fist. Macho spread himself thin. He became fully invested in the dope operations of Baltimore. In a matter of months, he was able to mostly lock down the slums, and place his troops in important regions of the city where the drug trade was the strongest. The Rebirth that his cousins were supplying him with was so potent that in a matter of days all the dope addicts that had partaken in the use of the drug were fully addicted and screaming for more.

Macho flooded the streets and beefed up his security. He greased palm after palm, and it became so that each police Patrol shift that worked his areas were making more working for him then they were for their departments. He kept them fed, just as much as he fed his animals. Macho knew money made the world go around, and if you didn't pay everybody around you. You would wind up on their plate sooner or later as the main entrée.

A month after the agreement to supply Angela Simms had gone into effect, he agreed to meet her at her home out in the Hamptons so they could discuss the furtherance of his business ventures. Macho was looking to move his hustle up and down the East coast and because Angela Simms was so powerful and well connected out East he knew she would be instrumental in helping him venture out of Baltimore. So, when she sent her Private Jet, he jumped on it and kicked back after giving Preston specific orders on how to keep all their operations afloat.

***

Macho's plane touched down early Saturday morning just as the sun was coming up. It landed with a loud screeching of the tires. Minutes later he was grabbing his Gucci luggage, and hopping onto the pavement. He handed his bag to the limo driver and slid into the stretch Bentley truck and was surprised to find Angela Simms already sitting inside it.

"You surprised to see me?" she asked lowering her glasses on her nose, looking over the rims at him. She was wearing a tight Burberry skirt dress that was so short most of her thighs were on display. Her curly hair set on her shoulders full of sheen. She had accentuated her eyes by use of mascara, and eyeliner. She was set up for the prowl.

Macho played it cool. "Yo', it's even better that you are. I got a lot of business to tend to back home so maybe we can spend the block a few times and I can get back?" He closed the door and pulled a bottle of Ace of Spades from the bucket of ice she had sitting next to her tucked in the console. The limo pulled off.

Angela laughed. "Why do I feel like I make you nervous, Macho?"

He popped the cork and drank directly from the bottle. "Shid I don't know. Only you can answer that question but I'm good."

She moved so that she sat directly across from him. Her short skirt rose higher on her frame. She crossed her thick, golden thighs. "Well, maybe my senses are off, but I highly doubt that. However, I feel you're going to make more money from this trip then you will from any other in your life. I mean as long as you play your cards right." She took the bottle from him and drank out of it. Licking around the rim of it with her pierced tongue.

Macho nodded his head. "Oh, so that's what you think, huh?"

"That's what I know, but you will soon find out. Just sit back and roll." She opened her thighs wide showing him that she was without panties. Her sex lips were thick and pudgy. She crossed her thighs again, looking into his eyes.

LaShawn came to Macho's mind immediately. He wondered if she was okay and if his security team had her fully covered? Ever since she'd told him what had transpired between her and Pooh two weeks prior, he'd been on high alert and worried about leaving her presence. Had Pooh not skipped town for business when he did Macho was sure he would have killed him already. He kept trying to keep Lashonda at the forefront of his brain. He didn't want to kill her father unless he really had too.

"Alright, Angela, we gon' play things yo' way. But I can't stay past tomorrow afternoon, and this shit better be beneficial to the God. Word up."

Angela felt her juices flowing. She liked how Macho talked to her as if she wasn't as powerful as she was. She was accustomed to men fawning all over her or bowing down to her because they knew how far her arm reached in the . It was irritating whereas Macho acted like she was an average hood chick.

"You know Macho I promise you that by the time you leave me, you will be all the way up, but you can help fulfill that promise by telling me what you are really looking for here?"

"Growth and expansion, I wanna move my Cutthroat Mafia into Philly, New York, Washington D.C, and even a few of the smaller cities. The ultimate goal is to have as many ma'fuckas trapping for me as possible. And of course, I'ma need protection to make it all work out. I ain't shy about greasing the palm of a pig but I think sooner or later I'ma need a politician, at least two, maybe a couple of judges as well. Can you help me with that?"

She nodded. "I have twelve judges, eighth senators, and more than a few lower-level politicians. I can help you out with this. As far as your expansion goes, your product is good. You will be able to easily move into one city after the next. There are gatekeepers in place in each major city but a head nod from me and you will get clearance. I'm willing to do all of this for you."

"And what will I have to do for you?" Macho snatched the bottle from her hand.

She snickered and lowered the partition. "Zeke, take us to the mansion. Get us there as soon as possible, it's urgent."

"Yes, ma'am."

***

Preston helped Kayley lay down on the bed. He kneeled beside her and filled his hands with Gold Bond Cocoa Butter lotion. He rubbed them together before applying it to her belly. Her chocolate stomach had a slight bulge, it was cute to him.

"This my baby belly, right here. Daddy gotta make sure I keep it free of those stretch marks. I don't want you being all insecure and stuff." He laughed.

Kayley mugged him. "I been puking up my guts every morning making room inside my body for your child that's guaranteed to have a big head like you, knowing I'm about to wreck my most sacred place. And you're worried about stretch marks, really?"

Preston backed away from her and held his hands slightly over her belly. "Yo', them hormones kicking yo' ass girl. You know damn well I'm just playing."

“Well, it’s not the right time. I feel up, and then I feel down. I keep having nightmares about Marco, and I'm worried about how we're going to raise this child. Are you absolutely sure we are ready?” She scooted back and fluffed her pillow behind her.

Preston got on the bed and sat beside her. He rested his left hand on her stomach rubbing the lotion into her skin. “I got you, Boo. I will never not have you. I think that us having this baby is a blessing. We can never be fully ready for it, but we have to take this one day at a time. That's all we can really do. I got your back, Kayley. As long as you have mine, we don't have to worry about anything. Me and the homie are knee-deep in the game now.” He leaned down and kissed her stomach.

“That's what I am worried about, Preston. You see that is not meant to be for the long term. It is always short-lived. My uncle thought he could survive in the game for a while and wound up getting indicted and losing his life to the Feds before he had the chance to enjoy all the money he had saved from trapping. I saw so many crazy things throughout my life. Baby I don't want us to be a part of this dope game forever. I know we can do better than it. We just have to believe that we can, then actually go out and do it. Like, if you couldn't be trapping what else would you want to do?”

“I don't know, Kayley. The money is good, we stacking that shit up like crazy. We’re about to move you from this apartment so we can have our own house on Hillcrest. I'm reaching for my sister, my niece. My mother thinking about coming around and going to rehab. Yo’, I couldn't do none of this shit if I wasn't out there trapping with Macho. So, I don't know what the fuck I would do if I wasn't. I just wanna provide for my people, that's it.”

Kayley scooted over to him and held his face in her hands. They felt warm to Preston. The scent of her perfume was soothing. "Honey listen to me. I understand your motives, and I get what you are trying to do for everybody, but we have a baby on the way. You cannot stay in those streets forever and be a father. You have to give the game up and get on something else. It's imperative that you do. So, what else would you be willing to do because I refuse to take no for an answer?"

"I guess I always wanted to own businesses around the hood. Stores, nail salons, laundromats, things of that nature. And when I was little, and we kept getting evicted out of all our places I always said I wanted to buy an apartment building and make the rent for poor mothers that could barely afford to be there. So, I wanna do that, too."

"So, real estate is something you're considering, as well as running a small business. I can help you with that. It just so happens that your woman already has her real estate license and business degree. We're going to work on getting you both of those as well but until then we're going to start buying up property, and businesses. That will be our thing, and our exit out of the game. Making money is all about longevity, and prosperity. You can't have one without the other. Now, all we need to do is to set a timeline for your departure. That will start with me. Give me that laptop off my dresser. I'm about to see what's all for sale in Baltimore."

Preston got off the bed, grabbed her laptop and handed it to her. "Kayley, on a serious note, only a real woman can snatch her man out of the game before it succumbs him. So, I just wanna let you know that I love and appreciate you for this. And I'm willing to listen." He kissed her lips.

She smiled and felt good to be appreciated. "Macho you belong to me and it's my job to see to it that our family is strong for a long, long time. Next, we gon' get your fine ass baptized." She smirked and was dead serious. "We can't accomplish nothing in life without God's covering."

"How about we do one thing at a time? You can't change a nigga all the way on the first day." He kissed her belly.

"I can't but, He can." She pointed toward the ceiling. "But it's cool we gon' take things one day at a time. Let's master this new hustle and allow the cards to fall where they may.

Chapter 15

It was ten-fifteen at night, and George was happy. He could finally shut the lights off in the store. He finished mopping up behind his meat section, and cleaned up the mop bucket, before putting it back. His stomach turned over and twisted in knots. His need for the dangerous Heroin was calling him and had been for two full hours but tonight was payday. He couldn't wait to get his pay. It was under the table just like he liked it.

He finished cleaning up what he had to and made his way to the front of the store where he gave it a once over to make sure nothing was out of place. After straightening a few things, he came from around the counter and made his way into the back of the store where Amir the store owner sat at his desk counting the funds from the day's take. He became anxious for his money. He tapped on the door to the office and came inside sitting across from Amir.

"Everything is done. I swept, I mopped, wiped down all the counters and put everything away. I'm ready to be paid so I can enjoy the rest of my night." He clapped and rubbed his hands together. He could already imagine what the night was about to be like.

Amir continued to count the money in front of him. He turned up his lip and frowned at George. "My father seems to think so much of you. He comes to this community and he wants to blend in so he hires an African instead of sticking with an Arab that he can trust. He thinks that if he hires somebody from your community things will go over well for his business and he will never have to worry about robbery or betrayal. But you and I both know that's bullshit now don't we, George?" Amir mugged him with hatred.

"What the fuck are you talking about, Mane? I've done my work, now I wanna be paid. It's time." He pointed at the palm of his hand. "Show me the money."

"Who were the men that beat up and robbed my father a few months ago while I was back in Jordan?" Amir balled his fist. He could feel his anger coursing through him.

"Say, Kid, I don't know what the fuck you're talking about. I wanna get paid so I can go out and party. All this other shit you are talking about is for the birds. Pay me and talk later."

"You know the men who robbed this store because after they robbed us you had a conversation with them. Then they played things off by beating you up a bit. But by that time, you three were already exposed. So, who were these men, and where are they now?"

George stood up. "You sitting yo' ass there talking about robbery when all you are doing is robbing me. Where is my muthafuckin' money man? I done *bussed* my ass for you for two weeks. Give me what I got coming."

Amir sat back in his seat and interlocked his fingers over his stomach. "In Jordan, a man that steals from a friend is considered a snake, or the devil. Your hands would be cut off. You would be stoned to death as you should. Since we came to this neighborhood we have been nothing but good to you people. In America you blacks are considered the sewer rats of the land, yet, we chose to mingle with you and to give your community a store built on principle and peace. You and your friends have corrupted what we have tried to do out of respect and friendship. Somebody has to pay the consequences for this betrayal. It will either be you, George or them. Who are you choosing? I need to know now."

George eyed Amir closely to see what angle he could play. He felt the man was trying to feel him out. He didn't think Amir really knew all that he was making it seem as if he did for sure. He felt Amir was fishing. He wasn't about to expose his hands to him that easily. There had to be another way, he thought. “Look, Amir, I don't know what you're talking about? I would never betray you or your father. I appreciate everything both of you have done for me this far. But I don't appreciate you coming at me like I'm some kinda sucka or somethin’. Now give me what I got coming so I can be on my way.”

Amir sat forward with a solemn smile on his face. He reached across the desk with blazing speed and slapped George so hard it sounded like thunder in the room. George fell out of the chair. Two Arabs dressed in all black appeared from the hallway with their faces fully covered by black cloths. They snatched George up and held him against the wall of the office.

Amir stepped in front of him. “Tell me who robbed our store and thought it was wise to put their hands on my father?” He cocked back his fist and slammed it as hard as he could into George's gut.

George doubled over and gagged. He felt like throwing up. He struggled to get loose. “Let me go man. I already told you I don't know what the fuck you're talking about. They were masked, I couldn't see their faces.”

Amir punched him in the gut two times really hard, and backhanded him? He spoke in Arabic. “This is why America treats you blacks like scum. You're untrustworthy. You're the scum of the earth. Even back home in Jordan, we think the same thing.” He punched him four hard times in the gut and took a step back.

Another Arab female entered the room wearing a black cotton dress and headpiece. She slowly walked to the desk with a tool kit in her hand. She placed it on Amir's desk and opened it. She was wearing long black leather gloves. She grabbed a pair of pliers out of the box and stepped in front of

George. Since she didn't know any English, she didn't waste time talking to him. She lifted George's shirt and latched the pliers on to his chest and pinched them together, pulling, and twisting them into a circle.

"Arrrrgh! Arrgh!" George was experiencing the worst pain in all his life. Tears began to flow from his eyes. "What the fuck is wrong with this, Bitch?" he hollered.

The Arab woman removed a large piece of skin and meat from his chest. She released it to the floor. Blood ran from the missing chunk in his chest. Before he could get used to the agonizing pain, she latched on again and pinched the pliers harder yanking downward.

George screamed like a little girl inside of a haunted house. He jumped into the air and bawled tears of agony. "Fuck this! Fuck this! I'll tell you! I'll tell you everything you need to know."

The Arab woman stepped closer to him and spat a loogey in his face. "You're a peasant," she said in Arabic. Then she walked away from him and stood behind Amir.

Amir rubbed a handful of salt into George's wounds causing him to scream once again. He slapped him across the face and grabbed him by the neck. "You're going to tell me everything you know about these bandits. When you're done, you'll pray to Allah that I spare your life."

***

Angela Simms stepped out of the hallway, into the living room where Macho sat on the couch smoking a Purple Haze stuffed Cuban cigar. He had the blunt in one hand, and a bottle of Cîroc in the other. Two of Angela's worker girls were giving him a massage and rubbing his chest simultaneously. Angela eased her way into the living room dressed in a short pink see-through Victoria Secrets negligee that showcased all her physical charms. She ran her tongue over her lips and sucked on the bottom one. She snapped her fingers for the girls to disappear. They followed her orders immediately. She looked down on Macho with a look of seduction.

"Do you like what you see?" Her right hand ran over the middle of her thighs, and up to the crease of her pussy. She was without panties.

Macho's eyes got bucked. He sat the bottle of champagne on the glass table, and the blunt in the ashtray after taking four quick pulls of it and inhaling hard. He blew the smoke to the ceiling. He was high as a kite and tipsy from the champagne laced with Mollie. "Yo', Shorty you look good as a mutha-fucka."

She laughed. "It's about time you noticed." She eased over to him and stood directly in front of him. "So, while you were in here being treated like a king. I was making a bunch of phone calls in your honor. I have your gateway to D.C, Philly, Brooklyn, and Charleston so far. These are some of the major cities on the East coast that could use your product and will help you get filthy rich in a matter of months. As long as you continue to allow me to work behind you. I can assure you that the dope game will be your Oyster."

Macho nodded. "It sounds like you been handling yo' bid-ness, and to what do I owe this pleasure?" His eyes gazed over her body. Images of LaShawn flashed into his mind. He grew weary and tried to shake the thoughts of her knowing what came next in order to further their lives.

Angela pulled up her negligee to show off her freshly shaved pussy, then straddled his lap. She held his face in her soft hands and looked into his eyes. "I want you, Macho. I like all that rough and rugged shit that you have going on, and I like the way that you do me."

Macho pushed her off his lap and stood up. "Bitch you think it's sweet? You ain't did shit for me that you ain't supposed to do for a Boss. This Baltimore's finest, right here. Word up."

Angela looked up at him with her knees in the sofa. She grew angry and stood up. "What?"

Macho took a hold of her hair and pulled her head backward making her yelp out in pain. He took her, slammed her against the wall and placed his hand around her throat. "Bitch, you heard me right." His left hand slipped between her thighs. Her pussy was dripping wet. He opened her lips and slid his middle finger into her crease.

"Yes, I heard you, Daddy." She tilted her head back.

"You think you the shit because you got a lil' pull, huh? Don't you know that I don't need nobody? I been getting this shit out the mud on my own, I don't need you." He slipped his finger in and out of her at full speed while thumbing her clitoris. He brought her to the brink of an orgasm sucking on her neck, and stopped, walking away from her.

Angela Simms shivered and tried to get a hold of herself. She walked over to him and fell to her knees. "I'll do anything for you, Macho, just tell me what to do. Keep treating me like you treating me and tell me what to do. I swear I'll do it." She rubbed the crotch of his pants and cuffed the log there. She trembled at the feel of how much meat Macho was working with.

Macho stared her down. "I ain't one of these average ass niggas. My dick ain't free, and you ain't just about to get it off yo' name. You gon' have to show and prove to me that you're worth me fucking the shit out of this pussy." He came to his knees, pushed her back, and tossed her right thigh on his shoulder. He rubbed her pussy for a brief second before three fingers invaded her womanhood, he stuffed them into her and thrust at full speed with no mercy.

"Unnhhh! Unnnhh! Unnhhh! Shit, Daddy—Daddy!" She cocked her thighs wide open for him. Her pussy was so wet that it seeped into her ass cheeks.

Macho thumbed her clitoris and went harder on his thrusting pressure. He began finger fucking her so hard and fast that his fingers became a blur going in and out of her. "Take this shit, Bitch."

"Uhhhh! Uhhhh! Fuck! Daddy I'm cumming! I'm cumming!" she screamed.

"Hell yeah!" Macho growled digging into her pussy. His hand was soaked and dripping off his wrists.

Angela Simms scooted backward and smacked his hand away. Her clitoris became too sensitive to touch. "Unnhh! Unhhh! Fuck!" She shivered with her pelvis inadvertently bucking forward.

Macho caught her, picked her up, and sat her couch. He pulled her over his lap and squeezed her fat booty. His hand raised in the air before he began to spank her like an unruly child. "This—what—you—gon—get—from—a—Boss." He spanked her harder and harder.

Angela Simms' eyes rolled into the back of her head. She felt like she was in sexual heaven. How did Macho know that she craved to be spanked? How did he know that being completely dominated would cause her to fall blindly in love? Her whole life she'd been given what she wanted because of her father being so high up in the game. Nobody had dared to tell her no or discipline her in any fashion, and she craved it. She didn't know where Macho truly came from, but she had no desire of ever letting him go.

Macho dug his fingers into her crease and went back to work in and out of her slit. She was dripping like he'd never seen before. “You love dis shit, Bitch, don't you? Don't you!” He slammed her harder.

Angela Simms panted and cocked her head back. “Awww fuck yeah!” She came with tears coming down her cheeks. She fell across his lap, then onto the floor with her thighs wide open. Her right hand played in her pussy. “Please fuck me, Macho. I'm begging you. If you fuck me, I will give you the world. Please.” She opened her lips wide to show him her pinkness.

Macho's dick was rock hard, but he had to keep LaShawn at the forefront of his brain. He had to be different for her. He stood up. “If you do everything you say you're gonna do then you'll get some of me. Until then, business is business.”

Angela jumped up and squeezed his dick through his jeans. She kissed the front of his pants. “I will, I swear to God I will. I got you, Daddy.”

Chapter 16

Three weeks after Kayley spoke about herself and Preston acquiring property to step outside of the drug game just a bit, she went into overdrive and had already found a slew of properties for sale. Ready to get Preston motivated on this new venture of thinking outside of the box she seized the properties immediately. It was three days after they'd bought them, and they were at the agency finishing up the signing of all the paperwork.

Kayley placed her hand on Preston's back as he signed the last bits of the necessary documents to finalize the buying of two apartment buildings of Guilford, one of the buildings housed Ilene, his mother.

"This is only the beginning, Baby. We're going to make our way through this town buying up as much of the condemned property as we can. I already have a nice amount of contractors ready to go in each building and get them up to code, and the people I am using are going to save us a lot of money. Everything is falling in place." She smiled and rested her hand on the top of her pregnant belly.

Preston finished signing everything and took a step back. He held up the paperwork to look it over one more time before he handed it to the female seller across from him. "Here you go, ma'am. It was nice doing business with you."

She smiled weakly. "You're welcome and have a nice day.

Kayley was trying her best to contain her excitement. She waited until they walked outside before she jumped into Preston's arms, and wrapped her legs around him. She kissed his lips happily. "I'm proud of us, baby. We are going to be unstoppable. I swear we are." She sucked all over his lips before he placed her down on her feet.

Preston held her face while the bright sunlight reflected off them. “Yo’, thank you, Goddess. I mean that. Just keep guiding me, and I swear I'ma take heed. You're my rib.” He kissed her forehead, then dropped down and did the same to her belly.

***

Later that night, Preston thought it would be special to surprise Ilene with a pop-up visit. He'd always had a key to her apartment, and this night he wanted to bring her a nice hot meal, and the good news that he was taking over her building, along with the one next to it. So, he slid the key in the lock and eased the door open. The first thing that hit him was the scent of funk and methamphetamine smoke. He curled his nose and stepped all the way inside of the apartment.

There were three men, along with Ilene and another female inside. One of the men had Ilene bent into a ball pounding her guts out with his dope dick. She groaned and whimpered as if she were in pleasurable pain. On the side of her was her friend and she was receiving the same treatment from a different dope addict. The last male was watching while he smoked methamphetamine from a glass pipe.

Preston dropped the bag full of KFC and cracked his knuckles. He snapped and went into action. He grabbed the man that was screwing Ilene off her and punched him so hard that the man was knocked out before he hit the ground. Preston stomped him six times in a row and kneed the dude that was fucking Ilene's friend in the temple. He knelt and pummeled him with blow after blow, then ran at the other man who jumped up and headed for the door. The man stopped and held up his guards. Preston didn't think nothing of it. He fired five quick blows, two of them landed in the man's nose and the last one broke it. Preston picked him up and dumped him on his neck.

He stood over him breathing hard. “Get y'all shit and get out of my mama crib! Now! Bitch you, too.” He pointed at Ilene's friend.

Everybody followed his orders, including the first man he'd knocked out. They slowly made their way past him groaning in pain. Now Preston had two pistols at his side, both were cocked. He was ready to kill something. He waited until the female came past him before he grabbed her by her nappy afro. She yelped.

“Bitch, if I ever see you around my mama, or this building again you gon’ be sorry. I promise you that. Take yo’ sick ass out of here and never come around my mama again. You hear me?” He tightened his grip on her hair.

“Yes.” She was in pain.

He tossed her out of the apartment and slammed the door. He gazed across the room at Ilene? She was putting her jogging pants on without underwear. Next came her sweater. She was embarrassed and ashamed at being caught. She refused to look Preston's way. He came and stood in front of her.

“Before you say anything lil’ boy you better remember that I am your mama. You don't run me, and I don't owe you no explanations. This is my house.” She scratched her dry scalp and walked past him into the kitchen. “You ain't have to beat them, men, up like that either. You ain't nothing but a bully.” She was higher than ever. The Rebirth flowed through her bloodstream.

Preston walked into the kitchen. “What's your problem, huh? Are you giving up on life?”

Ilene opened her refrigerator, four roaches crawled out of it and went into different directions. She took a half drank glass of Apple juice out of it and sipped from it. “I been gave up, ain't no reason for me to keep holding on, Preston. I'm tired of fighting." She walked back past him again and into the living room. She sat on the couch, crossing her thin thighs.

Preston picked up the bag of food and placed it on the table. A circle of roaches had already formed around it. Three mice ran from under the table, and into the kitchen. The table had food stuck to it, along with drug paraphernalia.

He shook his head. "Mama, why are you giving up?"

"I don't see no reason to keep fighting so I'ma do what I been doing until my clock runs out. Is that okay with you?"

Preston came and squat down in front of her. There was a bloodstain by his left foot from where one of the men that he'd gotten ahold of had bled. "You already know that's not okay with me and I refuse to accept that statement. I love you, and you mean the world to me. I need you here just so I can have the strength to think outside of the box. Mama your son is about to do some great things. I need your support more than ever." He rubbed the side of her face.

Ilene closed her eyes. "Boy, you don't need me. Everything you're doing out there is because of you. I been doing my own thing and that's what I'ma keep doing."

Preston held her shoulders and looked in her face. It was wrinkled and sunken. It had never been as dirty. She smelled like funk, fish, and must. It tore his heart, but she was still his mother. He loved her and felt like he needed her in his life in order for life to make sense. "My Queen please tell me what's wrong? I need to know because there is something going on inside of you that doesn't go unnoticed on your surface. I am your baby, talk to me."

"Why, Preston!" She jumped up. "Ain't nothing you can do to save me." She felt a sharp pain shoot through her stomach. She ignored it and struggled to breathe. She walked away from him and stood by the window. "This world ain't full of nothin but pain. I hate it. Anytime you trust somebody to have your best interest at heart they don't do nothin' but let you down. Well, it is what it is." She hugged herself and smiled. "At least I never gotta worry about being high no more. My baby run Baltimore. Good for you." She turned her back to him and pulled the blinds of her apartment so that everything went dark.

Preston came behind her and slid his arms around his mother holding her in protection. "Who hurt you, mama? Please tell me, and respect me enough to let me know what's going on with you? You're my heart and soul."

Ilene melted. "You were always a good kid, Preston. Boy always been crazy about his mama. I love that shit. Always been my lil' protector, but my baby ain't so little now, is he?" She laughed for a moment and then sighed. "You gotta promise me that you aren't going to do anything stupid." She turned around so that she was facing him. Her funk was heavier now because she was sweating at the thought of telling him what he was requesting of her.

"I've never lied to you as long as I have been alive and I ain't about to start now. You're my mother and my heart. Tell me what's good, right now." He held her face in his hands softly.

"I never meant to hurt your sister, or to do anything that would go against our family, but this drug makes me weak. It causes me to do things that I would never necessarily do if I didn't need it or was addicted to it. But I fuck up, Baby. I fuck up a lot. And I didn't mean to let that boy do to me what he did, but I did, and he gave me HIV. Now I can't get rid of it."

Preston released her. "He what? Who the hell are you talking about?"

"Pooh, Lashonda's father. That boy caught me many times in my weakness, and we slept together. He made me do a slew of sick things, too. I don't know why he craved me so much."

Preston fell backward until he wound up sitting on the couch. He lowered his head and tried to process the information she'd given him. "Mama are you sure it was him? It didn't come from nobody else, or sharing needles? I just saw you fucking that dope head without a rubber. Was you doing that before?"

"Pooh was the first man I slept with for a long time after me and your father split. I left your father physically healthy, yet mentally weak. I slept with Pooh for three months straight, only him. I found out what he'd given me in the second month. He admitted it to me after the doctors had already confirmed that I had it."

"And you kept sleeping with him?" Preston was shocked and appalled.

"He kept me high, that was enough for me."

Preston stood up. "I'ma kill this nigga. I'ma kill this nigga for taking my mama away from me." He was so mad that he felt hot. He was shaking.

Ilene opened the bag of KFC and took a drum stick out. She broke a piece off it and ate it. "It is written. Before that boy gave me that disease it was written. I just got what I had coming to me."

***

Later that night just before eleven, Preston pulled into the back of LaShawn's apartment. She stepped out of the building and jogged to his truck. She opened the door and jumped inside of it. Her security detail watched from a distance. They had already been given the word that Preston was coming, and he was given a pass to get as close to LaShawn as he was while Lashonda was inside being watched by Macho.

"Boy, what the hell is so important that you couldn't tell me over the Portal?" She hugged him and sat back in her seat worried about what he was getting ready to say.

Preston's eyes were still red. His lids were sore from wiping them so much. He felt weak and drained. "I gotta kill, Pooh."

"What, why? I mean not that I care or anything." She was at a fifty-fifty.

"His sick ass gave mama HIV. That's why she been going so hard on this dumb shit. She got that pack and she's dying. Pooh gave it to her right after she broke up with Pops. I hope you ain't been fucking that nigga."

LaShawn's eyes got to racing from side to side. Her stomach dropped. She had never felt sicker. "Are you serious lil', bruh? How the fuck did she and Pooh wind up getting together?" LaShawn was a bit jealous, then she snapped out of it. Her health came into play. "HIV, though?"

"You been fuckin that nigga, huh?" He grabbed her shirt and pulled her to him. "LaShawn, I swear to God I'll kick yo' ass if you have been. I'm already about to lose my mama, I can't lose my sister, too."

"Ain't nobody been screwing him. So, let me go."

Two of LaShawn's security members appeared on each side of the truck. They were armed and ready to unload on Preston if need me. They had been given the order from Macho to kill anybody that posed a threat to LaShawn. It didn't matter who the person was.

Preston released her. LaShawn waved them away. They backed up a few feet and kept their eyes on the pair. Preston was so drained that he didn't have the energy in him to snap out. "I still think you should get tested. You can never be too careful. Please, big sis."

She nodded. "I will, I still can't believe she would sleep with him, though." LaShawn became terrified. She tried to think about the last time that she and Pooh had gotten down. She couldn't think of it. "When did mama say she found out he gave it to her, was this recent?"

"Right after her and pops broke up. It had to be at least a year ago so if you been with him anything after that we should be worried." He sighed. "I gotta go, Kayley blowing me up. I love you, and I'll see you tomorrow, Lord willing."

She nodded, she leaned across this console and kissed his cheek. "Preston let me holler at Macho about this. I don't need you doing it for me. I got this. Promise me you'll give me that right."

"Why would Macho care about this? It ain't his business. What because he got you a little security, he got a stake on you now?" Preston was getting heated.

LaShawn saw where things were going and backed out. "I love you, Preston, have a good night."

"Yeah you, too."

She stood there after he pulled out of the parking lot stuck. She suddenly felt sick on the stomach and lost. She prayed that Pooh had not given her anything. She stood there for a while until she allowed her security to lead her back into her residence.

Chapter 17

Macho dropped the top of his black Porsche and stepped on the gas pushing the speeds to a hundred miles an hour. His dreadlocks were freshly twisted, they blew in the wind. He drank from a gold bottle of Rosé. He had a fully automatic Draco on his lap, and he was feeling like a champion. He glanced over at a quiet Preston and frowned. He'd been quiet for over ten minutes. Macho could tell something was plaguing him.

"Dawg what the fuck is the matter with you? You been quiet as hell for the longest." Macho switched lanes on the highway and stepped on the gas again sending up exhaust.

"Slow yo' ass down, nigga. You gon' fuck around and get us pulled over. I ain't finna go back to jail fucking with yo' crazy ass. Slow down," Preston demanded.

"Fuck that, I know you ain't ready to die. You have a baby on the way. You're in love with, Kayley, and shit is going good. You're planning on living life to the fullest, and because you are, I know you are less likely to try anything crazy with me speeding down the coast like this. So, I wanna tell you what's on my heart, and you better hear me out before you go nuts."

Preston braced himself in his seat. "Nigga, if you get me killed today, I swear to God I'm gon' kick your ass wherever we wind up whether it's heaven or hell. Now slow this fucking car down, and holler at me."

Macho switched lanes and kept at the same speeds. "Preston, I done had a cold heart ever since I was twelve years old. I been murdering ma'fuckas ever since I was thirteen, and that shit comes natural to me because my heart is so cold." He navigated the Porsche, and zoomed in front of a big semi-truck, and hit the gas again. "The only person that has ever been able to warm this cold ass heart is you because you are, my nigga, and LaShawn because I been in love with her ever since I first laid eyes on her. I don't see nobody but her. I need you to accept that. I'll kill for your sister, Preston. I want her to be my wife. I'm asking you for her hand, and I ain't taking no for an answer."

It took Preston's brain a second to register what Macho was saying. When it finally clicked, Preston's eyes got huge. "You mean to tell me that you and LaShawn been fucking around?" He turned to Macho ready to choke him out.

Macho stepped his foot on the gas and started to weave in and out of traffic. "I love her, Preston! That's my baby! I would never let nothin' happen to her or Lashonda. I need your blessing!" He floored the whip and pushed it past a hundred and ten miles per hour. It took off like a rocket. The wind blew in their faces and made their jaws wave like flags.

Preston sat back in his seat with his mind reeling. "That's why you gave her all those killas for security, huh?"

Macho nodded. "That's my jewel. I need to know she is well-protected at all times, only the best for her."

"And the new house she's moving into Thursday. You bought her that as your woman and not your sister, huh?" Preston hollered.

"A queen shouldn't be living in the ghetto. She is the best, so she's supposed to have the best at all times. I just wanna make her happy." Macho swerved slightly after shooting the Porsche in front of a red Benz Truck. He stepped on the gas again and the steering wheel began to shake. He'd topped a hundred and fifteen miles an hour.

"Macho, if my sister loves you as much as you do her, then you got my blessing. Now slow yo' ass down before you kill us," Preston warned.

"Really, you're giving me your blessing? All shit!" He eased his foot off the gas. The speed began to decelerate until it reached ninety-five when it hit ninety-three, they flew past a state patrol, and he clocked their speeds before he turned his sirens on. Macho looked over his shoulder. "Aw shit, Bruh."

Preston lowered his head. He had two forty Glocks on him, and a half brick of The Rebirth he was getting ready to drop off to one of his trap houses when Macho rolled up on him and told him to get inside his whip because they supposedly needed to talk. "Bruh, I'm dirty ass a Bitch. You gotta lose these ma'fuckas or we booked. Damn, something told me not to be fucking with you today."

Macho downed a nice portion of the champagne and stepped on the gas while he switched gears. The Porsche shot off like a rocket once again. He checked his rearview mirror and saw that they were leaving the highway patrol car in the dust. He swerved in front of a few cars and maintained his speed. They zoomed past another highway patrolman. His lights activated and he began to chase them. Macho felt amped up.

Preston was sick, he imagined sitting back in federal prison. He thought about the sound of the metal doors slamming, then standing for count. He imagined the rifle tower and became so sick that he felt like throwing up. "You better lose these ma'fuckas, Kid, word to God man."

Macho was already on it. He got off on the exit of Colgate and zipped past the traffic lights. He slowed his speed. When he came to the first alley, he turned into it and punched the accelerator. Rocks flew up into the air. He made a hard right at the end of the alley and took two side streets. They could hear the highway Patrol's sirens in the back of them. Macho dipped through another alley on Dixon and came out of it rolling over a pair of railroad tracks. He made a left onto Potomac Avenue's one way and made another left into another alley.

"Get out dawg. Take that dope and these guns and bounce. If I don't hit you up in two hours that means they got me. Come and bail me out. Now go!"

Preston grabbed the duffel bag and stuffed it with the guns. He slammed the door. "Nigga I love you dawg, and you got my blessing. Loose they ass B, word to the heavens." Preston took off running.

Macho smashed the gas and made haste out of the alley. He made a right and flew back down Colgate Street flying right past two highway patrol cars. He laughed and held up his middle finger. "Ma'fucka rolling a Porsche, why the fuck wouldn't I put you, bitches, to work. Come and get some!" He hollered and wound up right back on the expressway headed in the opposite direction from whence he came. By the time the highway patrol got back onto the expressway, Macho was long gone to his retreat. He laughed the whole way texting Preston that he was good with one hand.

***

"Hold ya horses. Here I come!" Ilene hollered as she walked up to her front door to answer it. She was jolted awake by the beating on the door. She looked through the peephole and saw LaShawn with her arms folded in front of her. She sensed trouble. She didn't feel like going there with her daughter. She put the chain on the door and opened it. "Girl what do you want? I got company," she lied.

"Who is it, Pooh?" LaShawn balled her hand into a fist and hit the door hard with it. "Open this damn door mama."

Ilene backed up. "Listen, Baby, I take it you spoke to Preston. Listen, I don't feel like doing this, right now. I don't feel good. If you will come back later, maybe we can talk about this then. Okay, sugah?"

LaShawn crashed into the door with her hip and broke the chain. It hung by the door with a piece of wood from the door attached to it. "Stop playing with me so ma'fuckin' much. I'm not a child anymore."

Ilene looked at the state of her front door and grew heated. "Bitch, you done broke my gotdamn lock. I hope you know you are paying for that shit, too. How dare you?"

"Why mama? Why did you sleep with my baby daddy behind my back?" LaShawn felt her heart breaking again.

"Because I couldn't do it in your face. I don't think you woulda let that happen." She snickered.

Whap!

LaShawn slapped Ilene across the face so hard it split Ilene's lip on the corner of her mouth. Blood dripped off her chin and on to her dirty sweater. "I'm not here to play these fuckin' games with you woman! You told my brother that Pooh gave you HIV. You think that's somethin' to play with?"

Ilene backed away from LaShawn holding her mouth. "You think it's okay for you to put your hands on me, huh? What you think just because I'm using that makes me less of your mother? I was in labor for twenty-two hours with you, LaShawn." She broke down to her knees crying. "I'm sorry, Baby. Lord knows I am. I shoulda never let that boy cum in me. I knew better but I allowed him to do me anyway. I'm so sorry. You have to believe me." She burst out crying.

LaShawn stepped up to her. "Every man I have ever been with has treated me like shit. They lied, they cheated, they stole from me. They never saw how precious, and rare I really was, until now. Now I have a man that is ready to die for me.

One that gives me the world and promises to do this for the rest of our lives, and I might not be able to have him anymore because of what Pooh might've gave me. All along you knew he had it, and you didn't tell me shit! Mama, you're ruining my life! Why would you do this to me? How could you?"

"I ain't perfect, I done made a whole lot of mistakes. I wish I didn't, but I did." She shook her head with her chin brushing up against her chest. "That boy dangled that dope in front of me and I just went. I had to have it. It ain't have nothing to do with your little selfish ass."

"*Selfish*? Did you just call me selfish? How fuckin' dare you?" She walked up on her mother and felt violent. She had never hit her before, but she felt like doing it right then.

"Your father gave you all his attention. He treated you better than he did me, and because he did our relationship went in the dumps real fast, especially when things went South for us because of our addictions. The only person he looked to make things right with was you," she grunted.

"So, you screwed my daughter's father to get back at me for the attention that my father showed me? You're sick. That's literally something a sick person would do."

"Well, I guess I am then. It don't help that your nasty ass baby father done made me a whole lot sicker. But anyway, what brings your angry ass over here tonight? You coulda at least had the decency to call me first."

"I just wanted to know if it was true? But I see that it is, and I don't have nothing else to say to you. You broke my heart. I just want you to know that you have never been a good mother. Ever since I was a little girl all you've ever done is hurt me one way or the other. I pray that I don't have what you have, but if I do, I plan on giving my daughter the best years of my life that I do have left. Thank you for nothing. I hope God is merciful on your soul." LaShawn left Ilene's home with a clean heart and a renewed spirit. As far as she was concerned, she no longer had a mother. She couldn't wait until her test results came back so she could know if she was HIV positive or not. Every second without knowing the results felt like it was a second that was killing her.

***

Twenty minutes after LaShawn left her home, Ilene walked into the kitchen and grabbed a steak knife out of the drawer. She didn't wait, she didn't hesitate. She took the blade and slit her wrists as deep as she could, before sitting in the bathtub with the *O'Jays* music turned all the way up. She smiled and closed her eyes singing away to the tune. She couldn't wait to die. The thought of death felt like bliss to her.

Chapter 18

It was a gloomy, rainy day. The wind coasted through the cemetery fiercely. Lightning flashed overhead in preparation for the imminent storm that brewed inside the eerie dark clouds. Preston held LaShawn under his right arm close to his body. It was the day of Ilene's burial and all the regular guests had already disappeared from the service. Preston kissed LaShawn on the forehead. He was struggling with mixed emotions.

On one hand, he felt pained that for the rest of his life he would be without his mother physically. He would miss holding her in his embrace and seeing her smile. Her laugh would often brighten his moods when he found himself in a dark one. A casual gesture of love from her would stick with him for weeks at a time. Though she was going through her own set of struggles she had been his heart and soul, and he would miss her dearly.

On the other hand, Preston felt that it may have been time for his mother to go back to the Lord. Not only was she struggling with a serious addiction to Heroin, and other drugs that he didn't even know about, she was also dying from HIV, and had refused treatment for her disease. In his book, she was ready to go, and her taking her own life may have been a vindication of exactly that.

"Preston, I don't know how to feel." LaShawn looked up at Preston with a blank expression on her face. "I mean I'm sorry she's dead, but on the other hand, I feel like she was dead way before life left her body. I didn't even love her no more."

Preston held her tighter. "Don't say that, sis. You don't mean that." He kissed her forehead again.

"The hell if I don't. I will never be able to forgive her for what she did to me. Not even in her death. Come on Lashonda it's about to pour down raining." She walked away from him and pulled her daughter along putting Lashonda's hood on for her.

Kayley stepped beside Preston and looked up at him. The rain began to fall heavily from the sky. "Baby are you ready to go, yet? It looks like it's about to get real bad out here." She pulled her hood more over her face.

Preston looked over at his mother's casket and shook his head. There was nothing more to say or do, Ilene was gone. The only person he had left was his father. That crushed his soul to even think about. "Yeah, Boo, let's get on up out of here. We need a few days away from Baltimore. It feels like this city is closing in all around me. I just need to lay up with my baby girl, you feel me?" His eyes remained on his mother's casket.

"I feel you, baby. I think you are right." She interlocked her fingers with his. "Let's get up out of here."

Preston stepped over and touched his mother's casket one more time. He opened it and took a deep breath before kissing her on the forehead. "I love you, Goddess. You will always be my life. Never forget that." He kissed her one last time and closed the casket back. The rain began to come down as hard as it ever had. He grabbed Kayley's hand and they slowly walked through the rain while she held her umbrella out for them. "Kayley I wanna spend the next two days catering to you, baby. I don't wanna think about the hood. I just wanna think about you and our child growing inside of you. Do you hear me, Precious?"

Kayley nodded and made it to the Range Rover first. Preston opened the door for her and allowed her to climb in the truck before he closed it back. Kayley reached over and opened his door before he got there. She worried about him and prayed that he would be stronger soon. The last week had been rough for him.

"Baby are you sure you don't need me to cater to you? I mean, after all, you're the one that just lost a parent. I wouldn't mind being your rock for a few days. We don't have to spend all thirty-six hours catering to me. I mean what else is a Queen for?"

"N'all baby, it's all good. You've been a champ this whole week. I need to focus on the more important things like you and our child. I mean I love you to death for wanting to continue to make things all about me, but it's your time, or should I say y'all turn," he spoke in terms of Kayley and their unborn child.

Kayley smiled and took a deep breath. "Well, I really do love you, and I am here for you. Always know that."

"I do." He started up the truck and pulled it away from the parking space with his head still spinning over the loss of his mother. He glanced over at Kayley and tried his best to seek strength from her presence. Life was precious, Kobe Bryant, Gianna Bryant, and now his mother put truth to that.

Kayley reached over and took a hold of his hand. She slid her fingers inside of his. "So, what do you wanna do first when we get to this resort?"

"Honestly, I just wanna chill, cater to you, and get me some of that pregnant pussy." He stuck his tongue out at her.

She pursed her lips. "Unhhh! Unhhh, the first thing you need to know when it comes to a woman is that we are physical last, and emotional first. If you are planning on making this three-day vacation all about me, you need to know I will desire for you to feed my emotions, and for you to cater to my mind. That's how you can spoil me."

"Oh, yeah, well I think I might be feeling a little more depressed than I thought. Maybe we should make this vacation all about me. Why not?"

She rolled her eyes and shook her head. "Yeah, right, you've already missed that window of opportunity." She giggled. "But for real though, Preston, I just wanna vibe these few days. We can get down but let that be the end result of our coming into our oneness. Cool?"

"Cool?" Preston looked over at her for a moment. It had gotten pitch black outside. The rain was coming down terrible, popping against the windshield of the truck like hail. "I really love you, Kayley. Yo', and I ain't never been in love with no female before."

"Why is that? What, you was too strong to fall in love or something?"

Preston shrugged his shoulders. "I don't know. I guess I just never felt that way about a female before. I didn't trust women because I grew up watching my mother do a lot of shiesty things in honor of her drug addiction. Also, she and my father's relationship was so toxic. They were always fighting, or arguing, or doing something that just told me women and men weren't supposed to be together for a long time. So, I never allowed myself to fall for anybody, until you."

"Then, why me? And I mean other than us saving each other's lives? Is there something special about me?"

"Everything is special about you. The way you are. Your skin color, your voice, your smell. The way you make me feel. How you make me want to better myself for the future and for those that are under my domain. Yo', you put fat on my brain. Any nigga that ain't trying to hear his Rib out is a goof. Word to God man. A man has a woman as his equal for a reason. Y'all help us see beyond the surface of impulse and manly blindness. I needed you, and now that I got you, I will never let you go because you are my completion."

Kayley hated getting emotional, but she couldn't help it when Preston said the things he was saying to her. "Baby just know that just as priceless as I am, you are also, and you are a compliment to me as well. We love you, me and your child."

"And that's all that matters. Now let's go have us a nice three-day vacation. We deserve it."

***

Macho waited until LaShawn stepped out of the shower before he slid his arms around her waist and nestled his face into her neck. "Hey, baby, are you okay?"

LaShawn sighed, and her body went weak against the feel of his muscular chest. "I don't know how I feel, right now. I guess I feel more lost than anything. Here it is that I just buried my mother and I feel so cold toward her entire death. I think something might be wrong with me."

"You sure there isn't somethin' you wanna talk about?" Macho turned her around, so she was facing him.

LaShawn kept her head lowered, and felt her brain being bombarded with a thousand thoughts at once. She had to shake it hard in order to get some form of relief mentally. "I wanna tell you something Macho but I don't wanna freak you out. I also don't want you getting mad about what I am going to tell you, please, because that is the most important part."

Macho ran his fingers through her hair in order to get it out of her face. He stroked her cheek looking into her eyes. She was so precious to him. "Baby you can tell me anything. I promise I won't get mad. Come on." He took ahold of her hand and walked into their bedroom. He led her to the big bed and sat beside her. "Go ahead lil' baby, I'm listening."

LaShawn tried her best to build up the nerve so she could tell him everything she needed to. Macho was a damn good man and she didn't want to lose him. So many thoughts began running through her mind of how things could go between them that before she opened her mouth, she became defeated. She didn't know where to start, or what to say period. She started to feel sick, and a bit woozy. She was freaking herself out. She took a deep breath and blew it out.

Macho lowered his eyes and became troubled. The first thing he thought about was cheating. He figured LaShawn had stepped out on him when he mighta been out of town on business, but then he quickly dismissed it because wherever she went he made sure there was a plethora of security around her at all times. "Baby talk to me."

LaShawn closed her eyes and allowed her mind to stop racing. She took another deep breath, and slowly blew it out. "Okay, before my mother passed away, I found out a few things about her that has me mentally screwed up, right now. I am trying as best as I can to forgive her, but I am finding it so hard to do so—" She paused and imagined Pooh and Ilene together. It sickened her, she balled her hands into fists.

Macho rubbed her back and continued to look in her beautiful face. "Go ahead, baby, it's okay. I am here for you."

She nodded. "Well, first, my mother and my father had a very toxic relationship that was surrounded with drug and alcohol abuse. My father was a very violent man. And after a few years my mother became the same—" She paused again and struggled to breathe. Her emotions were getting the best of her. Tears ran down her cheeks, she wiped them away. "Needless to say their relationship became so violent that they didn't last very long. My father has put my mother in the hospital after breaking a bunch of her bones and when she came out, she left him and moved over to Guilford. I guess during the first few months of her breakup she musta been mentally fucked because she started creeping around with Lashonda's sperm donor."

"Pooh?" Macho was caught off guard. "Yo', Ms. Ilene used to mess with that nigga?"

LaShawn nodded her head. "Yeah, and I don't know if it was around the time when he and I were still together or not. But ever since I found out about it, I just been hating my mother and wishing her, and I were never related. But that's not the end of the story, Baby." She took a second to gather herself again. Tears were flowing freely out of her eyelids. "Baby before you and I got together, or I even knew that you wanted me as much as you did, Pooh came over to the house and forced himself on me. I fought him off as best as I could, but he got the better of me and he did his thing."

Macho jumped up. "What, did you tell Preston?"

She shook her head. "I didn't tell nobody because I know how crazy Pooh is. He woulda been trying to seek revenge against me. At that time, I didn't have all the security detail that you have set up for me, right now. But if I did I woulda told somebody."

"Fuck, I'm so sick of hearing that bitch ass nigga's name. He's always doing something. This shit is irritating." Macho needed to pace. He walked back and forth trying to calm himself down, but it wasn't working. "Yo', that's it LaShawn, I'm bodying this nigga. He been getting away with too much shit. The only reason I ain't smoked him yet is because of my respect for you and Lashonda. That's it." He punched his hand.

LaShawn got up. "Baby, it's okay. Please calm down and let me finish."

"N'all fuck calming down. This nigga is a thorn in my side. Now I gotta find out that he raped my wife to be, fuck that. Yo', I'm out of here, I need some air." He left out of the room with her calling his name. He stopped in his guest room where his guns were, and placed two .45s on his hip, along with a Kevlar bulletproof vest across his chest. He was angry and feeling like killing something. He kept on imagining Pooh forcing himself on LaShawn and the imagery was enough to make him go insane.

"I'm finna smoke this punk. That's gon' be that." He stormed out of the house with murder on his mind.

Chapter 19

Preston took the cherry-scented massage oil and dribbled it over Kayley's back. He took his big hands and massaged it into her smooth skin and kissed the back of her neck. "How are you feeling chocolate love?"

She smiled and kept her head laid on her arms. "I'm feeling like a bosset, just as long as you keep it up. Remember slow and steady wins the race." She snickered.

"Oh, slow and steady, huh?" He trailed his hands down her back, and cuffed her fat booty massaging the cheeks? He opened them so he could watch her chocolate pussy wink at him. Ever since she'd been pregnant, her pussy had gotten fatter and juicier. Preston trailed his fingers down the middle of her slit and tried to slide a finger into her center. He was thirsty for the feel of her hotness.

"Unnhhh." Kayley arched her back. "Unnhhh, unnhhh, Preston, you better get those fingers out of there. You promised you would make these three days all about me. That's about you."

Preston opened her cheeks and sucked her pussy lips licking his tongue up and down her slit. He swallowed her dew. "N'all I'ma chill, Baby, I just needed to taste my lil' pregnant woman for a second. You already know how them juices be having me." He kissed each ass cheek and rubbed up her body until he was massaging her shoulders again.

Kayley was already oozing between the thighs. "Now that's more like it." She smiled. "Can you tell me how beautiful I am?"

"No doubt, baby, I swear you are the most beautiful woman in this world to me. I love your chocolate skin and your Asian slanted eyes. You are gorgeous, I know that without a shadow of a doubt I can wake up to you happily for the rest of my life. When I look at you, I see my wife and the mother of my children. You are perfect, and I feel blessed to call you my own."

Kayley turned over on the massage table that came equipped with the Penthouse suite to look at him. "Aw baby, are you serious? Do you really feel that way?"

"Hell yeah, I do. You are my portion of Africa, and I worship you." He kissed her forehead.

"Damn, here we go with this shit. Now we supposed to be making this weekend all about me. But you already know when you get to talking like that what it does to me." She batted her eyelashes. "You still wanna worship me?" Her thighs slowly opened until she was revealing her trimmed pussy. She slid her left hand in between her legs and opened her sex lips. "Well, worship this temple then. What are you waiting for?"

Preston kissed down her body until he reached her opening. He kissed the lips there and slurped up the juices that were coming out of her crease. He swallowed and trembled from the taste of her in the back of his throat. "Baby, you sure you want me to do my thing, right now? You already know how I get when I get going."

"As long as you are worshipping me, then hell yeah. Baby, get that pussy. It's yours, until my last breath. Now get it!"

Preston dove face first, eating that pussy like a thirsty trained lesbian. He held her ass cheeks in his hands and went to work, rubbing his face from the side and sucking on each lip individually. He loved the taste of her. She had been the first female that he'd ever desired the taste of, and he honestly believed that it was because she was so Black. He loved her skin color and everything about her features.

Kayley cocked her thighs wide open and laid back on her elbows while Preston devoured her. Her baby bump slightly obstructed her view but not enough to block him completely.

She loved to watch Preston go to work. It drove her crazy to know that he desired her so much. She gasped and opened her mouth wide. She could feel him flicking against her clitoris with his tongue. Then he was sucking it like a berry. She arched her back hard and humped into his mouth. He opened her lips further and stuck his tongue as far into her as it could go. She lost it, she fell back and covered her face with her hands. The next thing she knew she was screaming at the top of her lungs.

"Aw, fuck! Fuck! Fuck! I'm cumming, Preston!" She pushed his face into her honeycomb and rode it until she began to quiver like crazy.

Preston slurped, licked and sucked. His neck was saturated with her juices. It ran down his collarbone, and onto his chest. His gold ropes became sticky. "That's my baby. This my baby, right here." He rolled his middle finger around her clit while she bucked up at him. He opened her sex lips and kissed her right on her pink before he slid up her body. "Baby, suck these juices off of my lips."

She took his head in both of her hands and licked all over his mouth. She sucked his top lip, then his bottom one. Next, her tongue was all over the lower portion of his face. That drove Preston crazy. She pulled him down between her thighs and wrapped her ankles around his waist. Her nails lightly trailed down his back.

"Preston, I am blessed to have you as well, Baby. I am thankful that God put us in each other's paths. Now that you and I have been together, I can't understand how I've ever been able to get by without you beside me." She kissed him and hugged his body to hers.

Preston slipped from the massage table and picked her up in his arms. He carried her to the big king-sized bed that was decorated with red and white rose petals. He laid her down on her side and scooted behind her. He held her possessively, rubbing her stomach. "Life is so crazy, Kayley. The way we met, how fast we've fallen for one another, and now with this blessing growing inside of you. I just want to do the best I can for you and our baby. I don't feel like I have any room to make any mistakes. I just wanna make you two proud." He kissed the back of her neck.

"Baby we already know that the odds are stacked against us. Based on your record, and where I come from the statistics say that we are doomed to fail. But that is why we have to fight harder and harder each day, and we have to stay united as one. We have to get you off those streets and in a real job. Since you're so used to the buying and selling of things, maybe it's meant for you to be a real estate agent. I can see you getting dressed for work every day to go to the office so you can make a bunch of deals and buy up a bunch of properties. I think that you are destined for greatness."

"I think that *we* are destined for greatness. I don't want to do nothing if it ain't benefitting you and my family. I got this, though. This shit gon' be hard because I am so used to fast money, but we got a nice amount of it put up. So, I think it's time to turn over a new leaf and conquer some things outside of the dope game. I ain't trying to see the inside of a Federal Courtroom again. The thought of it is terrifying to me." Preston's phone began buzzing like crazy, he tensed.

Kayley tapped him on the waist. "Leave it, baby. You said the next three days is supposed to be all about me. I'm laying right here. That phone ain't got nothing to do with me."

The phone buzzed again, Preston sat up. "Yeah, baby, but that is my special phone. The only time it's going to ring is if it is a severe emergency. There are only two people that has the number besides you, that's LaShawn and Macho. If either one of them is calling me that means its trouble. Please let me get it."

Kayley thought about it and began to imagine the worst-case scenarios. "Okay, go ahead."

Preston jumped up and grabbed his phone. He placed it on speaker right away so Kayley could hear. "What's good?"

"Preston, you gotta find Macho. He just stormed out of the house saying that he was going to take care of Pooh. I'm scared. I don't know what he about to do and I don't wanna lose my man," she sounded hysterical to him.

"Sis, how long ago was this?"

"A few hours. He ain't answering his phone, and I'm driving myself crazy with worry. Pooh, ain't answering his phone either and neither is Rickie. She was supposed to bring my daughter back home in the morning but now I'm feeling like I want Lashonda here tonight just so she's away from, Pooh."

"What the fuck is Macho wilding out about?" Preston was already getting dressed.

"I told him how Pooh raped me before he and I got together, and he snapped. Please go find him."

"Pooh did what!" Preston snapped.

"Not right now Preston, please. Just find my man." She disconnected the phone.

Preston looked over at Kayley. Kayley had her arms crossed in front of her. The expression on her face told him she didn't feel like hearing the bullshit. He stepped over to her and rubbed her stomach. He leaned down to kiss it.

"Five hundred a night. This room is costing us five hundred a night and you are about to go out and track down a grown ass man that don't got nothin' to do with you and I. Ugh." She laid on her side and pulled the covers that they'd brought with them over her head. "You better hurry yo' black ass back, Preston. Don't make me come looking for you."

Preston kissed her backside and grabbed his truck keys. "I love you, Kayley. I'll be back."

"I love you, too. Just hurry, I need you."

***

Amir and his crew of angry Arab killas watched Preston come out of the hotel and jump in his truck. They had been trailing him for three days now awaiting the right time to strike and make Preston pay for his transgressions against Amir's father. Amir smiled to himself after watching Preston leave the parking lot. He thought about the pregnant and vulnerable Kayley upstairs.

'*There was more than one way to break a man into a million pieces*,' he thought.

He glanced up at the hotel and slid his black gloves on his hands. '*Yeah, Preston had to pay big*,' were the only thoughts that bounced around in his mind.

***

Macho cruised with his Draco on his lap, and his head nodding to *Moneybagg Yo* coming out of his speakers. He'd been given a tip from one of the Guilford dope addicts that Pooh was in the area making a few drop-offs, and he was looking to catch him slipping. The dope addict said Pooh was traveling from trap to trap dropping off product and picking up his money as he went along. Macho thought it would be the night that he would get rid of the shiesty low life dope boy for good. He'd done too much wrong and had crossed too many lines for him to still be breathing.

Macho was wishing he'd taken care of Pooh a long time ago. He imagined Pooh forcing himself on LaShawn and the vision was enough to make him want to cry. There was no turning back, Pooh's ass was out.

***

Pooh stepped out of thirty-six nineteen apartment building and clutched his purple Crown Royal to his chest. It was filled with thirty thousand dollars in cash. It had been a good week for the complex. He strolled back to his G Wagon. It was three in the morning, and already he could tell it was set up to be a hot and muggy day. He got back to his Wagon and slipped into the driver's seat. He placed the bag in between the passenger and driver's seat.

He looked into his rearview mirror. Lashonda's face came into view. "Lil' mama are you okay back there?"

Her eyes had started to close. When she heard his voice, they popped back open. She yawned and stretched her arms above her head. Her knuckles scraped the roof of the Wagon. "I'm sleepy daddy, I just want to lay down."

Pooh started the Wagon. "Well, baby time is money. Daddy got a few more things to take care of, then I'll drop you back off at Rickie's unless you want me to take you home. Do you want to be around all of those sad funeral people?"

"No, I'm scared of dead people daddy. I just wanna stay with you." She reached her arms out for him.

"Baby, you gotta stay strapped in. It's only gonna be for a minute. Why don't you close your eyes just for a little while, okay?"

Lashonda didn't need to be told twice. She yawned and closed her eyes. "Okay, daddy." Before he pulled out of the space she was knocked out.

Pooh started the Wagon and sat there for a moment. He pulled a blunt out of the glove compartment and sparked it.

His console was full of bags of money. He nodded and inhaled the smoke. “I'm a muthafuckin’ boss.” His cellphone rang startling him. He reached over on the seat to retrieve it. He felt a tingle go down his spine. When he looked in the passenger's window he jumped back. He tried to reach under the seat for his pistol.

Macho wasted no time. He upped the Draco and began blasting on Pooh with no remorse or regard for his life. “Bitch ass nigga!” he hollered.

Pooh felt five slugs slam into him simultaneously. He threw the Wagon in drive and stepped on the gas. The Wagon took off. Macho kept shooting, chopping the Wagon down. The windows busted out, bullets slammed into the seats. Four more slugs caught Pooh. His foot punched the gas. The Wagon took off like a rocket across the parking lot where it slammed into a metal garbage can and blew up off impact. Pooh and Lashonda began to scream and holler. Macho rolled behind the Wagon, jumped out and kept firing until his gun was empty. Then he jogged away from the explosion and hopped into his truck with a smile under his mask.

To Be Continued...
Cutthroat Mafia 2
Coming Soon

Submission Guideline

Submit the first three chapters of your completed manuscript to ldpsubmissions@gmail.com, subject line: Your book's title. The manuscript must be in a .doc file and sent as an attachment. Document should be in Times New Roman, double spaced and in size 12 font. Also, provide your synopsis and full contact information. If sending multiple submissions, they must each be in a separate email.

Have a story but no way to send it electronically? You can still submit to LDP/Ca$h Presents. Send in the first three chapters, written or typed, of your completed manuscript to:

LDP: Submissions Dept
Po Box 870494
Mesquite, Tx 75187

DO NOT send original manuscript. Must be a duplicate.

Provide your synopsis and a cover letter containing your full contact information.

Thanks for considering LDP and Ca$h Presents.

Coming Soon from Lock Down Publications/Ca$h Presents

BOW DOWN TO MY GANGSTA

By **Ca$h**

TORN BETWEEN TWO

By **Coffee**

THE STREETS STAINED MY SOUL **II**

By **Marcellus Allen**

BLOOD OF A BOSS **VI**

SHADOWS OF THE GAME II

By **Askari**

LOYAL TO THE GAME **IV**

By **T.J. & Jelissa**

A DOPEBOY'S PRAYER **II**

By **Eddie "Wolf" Lee**

IF LOVING YOU IS WRONG… **III**

By **Jelissa**

TRUE SAVAGE **VII**

MIDNIGHT CARTEL III

DOPE BOY MAGIC III

By **Chris Green**

BLAST FOR ME **III**

A SAVAGE DOPEBOY III

CUTTHROAT MAFIA II

By **Ghost**

A HUSTLER'S DECEIT III

KILL ZONE **II**

BAE BELONGS TO ME III

SOUL OF A MONSTER III

By **Aryanna**

THE COST OF LOYALTY **III**

By **Kweli**

CHAINED TO THE STREETS II

By **J-Blunt**

KING OF NEW YORK V

COKE KINGS IV

BORN HEARTLESS IV

By **T.J. Edwards**

GORILLAZ IN THE BAY V

De'Kari

THE STREETS ARE CALLING II

Duquie Wilson

KINGPIN KILLAZ IV

STREET KINGS III

PAID IN BLOOD III

CARTEL KILLAZ IV

Hood Rich

SINS OF A HUSTLA II

ASAD

TRIGGADALE III

Elijah R. Freeman

KINGZ OF THE GAME V

Playa Ray

SLAUGHTER GANG IV

RUTHLESS HEART III

By Willie Slaughter

THE HEART OF A SAVAGE II

By Jibril Williams

FUK SHYT II

By Blakk Diamond

THE DOPEMAN'S BODYGAURD II

By Tranay Adams

TRAP GOD II

By Troublesome

YAYO III

A SHOOTER'S AMBITION II

By S. Allen

GHOST MOB

Stilloan Robinson

KINGPIN DREAMS II

By Paper Boi Rari

CREAM

By Yolanda Moore

SON OF A DOPE FIEND II

By Renta

FOREVER GANGSTA II

By Adrian Dulan

LOYALTY AIN'T PROMISED II

By Keith Williams

THE PRICE YOU PAY FOR LOVE II

By Destiny Skai

THE LIFE OF A HOOD STAR

By Rashia Wilson

TOE TAGZ III

By Ah'Million

CONFESSIONS OF A GANGSTA II

By Nicholas Lock

PAID IN KARMA II

By **Meesha**

I'M NOTHING WITHOUT HIS LOVE II

By Monet Dragun

CAUGHT UP IN THE LIFE II

By Robert Baptiste

NEW TO THE GAME II

By **Malik D. Rice**

Life of a Savage II

By **Romell Tukes**

Quiet Money II

By **Trai'Quan**

Available Now

RESTRAINING ORDER **I & II**

By **CA$H & Coffee**

LOVE KNOWS NO BOUNDARIES **I II & III**

By **Coffee**

RAISED AS A GOON I, II, III & IV

BRED BY THE SLUMS I, II, III

BLAST FOR ME I & II

ROTTEN TO THE CORE I II III

A BRONX TALE I, II, III

DUFFEL BAG CARTEL I II III IV

HEARTLESS GOON I II III IV

A SAVAGE DOPEBOY I II

HEARTLESS GOON I II III

DRUG LORDS I II III

CUTTHROAT MAFIA

By **Ghost**

LAY IT DOWN **I & II**

LAST OF A DYING BREED

BLOOD STAINS OF A SHOTTA I & II III

By **Jamaica**

LOYAL TO THE GAME I II III

LIFE OF SIN I, II III

By **TJ & Jelissa**

BLOODY COMMAS I & II

SKI MASK CARTEL I II & III

KING OF NEW YORK I II,III IV

RISE TO POWER I II III

COKE KINGS I II III

BORN HEARTLESS I II III

By **T.J. Edwards**

IF LOVING HIM IS WRONG…I & II

LOVE ME EVEN WHEN IT HURTS I II III

By **Jelissa**

WHEN THE STREETS CLAP BACK I & II III

By **Jibril Williams**

A DISTINGUISHED THUG STOLE MY HEART I II & III

LOVE SHOULDN'T HURT I II III IV

RENEGADE BOYS I II III IV

PAID IN KARMA

By **Meesha**

A GANGSTER'S CODE I &, II III

A GANGSTER'S SYN I II III

THE SAVAGE LIFE I II III

CHAINED TO THE STREETS

By J-Blunt

PUSH IT TO THE LIMIT

By **Bre' Hayes**

BLOOD OF A BOSS **I, II, III, IV, V**

SHADOWS OF THE GAME

By **Askari**

THE STREETS BLEED MURDER **I, II & III**

THE HEART OF A GANGSTA I II& III

By **Jerry Jackson**

CUM FOR ME I II III IV V

An **LDP Erotica Collaboration**

BRIDE OF A HUSTLA **I II & II**

THE FETTI GIRLS **I, II& III**

CORRUPTED BY A GANGSTA I, II III, IV

BLINDED BY HIS LOVE

THE PRICE YOU PAY FOR LOVE

By **Destiny Skai**

WHEN A GOOD GIRL GOES BAD

By **Adrienne**

THE COST OF LOYALTY I II

By Kweli

A GANGSTER'S REVENGE **I II III & IV**

THE BOSS MAN'S DAUGHTERS I II III IV V

A SAVAGE LOVE **I & II**

BAE BELONGS TO ME I II

A HUSTLER'S DECEIT I, II, III

WHAT BAD BITCHES DO I, II, III

SOUL OF A MONSTER I II

KILL ZONE

By **Aryanna**

A KINGPIN'S AMBITON

A KINGPIN'S AMBITION **II**

I MURDER FOR THE DOUGH

By **Ambitious**

TRUE SAVAGE I II III IV V VI

DOPE BOY MAGIC I, II

MIDNIGHT CARTEL I II

By **Chris Green**

A DOPEBOY'S PRAYER

By **Eddie "Wolf" Lee**

THE KING CARTEL **I, II & III**

By **Frank Gresham**

THESE NIGGAS AIN'T LOYAL **I, II & III**

By **Nikki Tee**

GANGSTA SHYT **I II &III**

By **CATO**

THE ULTIMATE BETRAYAL

By **Phoenix**

BOSS'N UP **I , II & III**

By **Royal Nicole**

I LOVE YOU TO DEATH

By Destiny J

I RIDE FOR MY HITTA

I STILL RIDE FOR MY HITTA

By **Misty Holt**

LOVE & CHASIN' PAPER

By **Qay Crockett**

TO DIE IN VAIN

SINS OF A HUSTLA

By **ASAD**

BROOKLYN HUSTLAZ

By **Boogsy Morina**

BROOKLYN ON LOCK I & II

By **Sonovia**

GANGSTA CITY

By **Teddy Duke**

A DRUG KING AND HIS DIAMOND I & II III

A DOPEMAN'S RICHES

HER MAN, MINE'S TOO I, II

CASH MONEY HO'S

By Nicole Goosby

TRAPHOUSE KING **I II & III**

KINGPIN KILLAZ I II III

STREET KINGS I II

PAID IN BLOOD **I II**

CARTEL KILLAZ I II III

By **Hood Rich**

LIPSTICK KILLAH **I, II, III**

CRIME OF PASSION I II & III

By **Mimi**

STEADY MOBBN' **I, II, III**

THE STREETS STAINED MY SOUL

By **Marcellus Allen**

WHO SHOT YA **I, II, III**

SON OF A DOPE FIEND

Renta

GORILLAZ IN THE BAY **I II III IV**

DE'KARI

TRIGGADALE I II

Elijah R. Freeman

GOD BLESS THE TRAPPERS I, II, III

THESE SCANDALOUS STREETS I, II, III

FEAR MY GANGSTA I, II, III

THESE STREETS DON'T LOVE NOBODY I, II

BURY ME A G I, II, III, IV, V

A GANGSTA'S EMPIRE I, II, III, IV

THE DOPEMAN'S BODYGAURD

Tranay Adams

THE STREETS ARE CALLING

Duquie Wilson

MARRIED TO A BOSS… I II III

By Destiny Skai & Chris Green

KINGZ OF THE GAME I II III IV

Playa Ray

SLAUGHTER GANG I II III

RUTHLESS HEART I II

By Willie Slaughter

THE HEART OF A SAVAGE

By Jibril Williams

FUK SHYT

By Blakk Diamond

DON'T F#CK WITH MY HEART I II

By Linnea

ADDICTED TO THE DRAMA I II III

By Jamila

YAYO I II

A SHOOTER'S AMBITION

By S. Allen

TRAP GOD

By Troublesome

FOREVER GANGSTA

By Adrian Dulan

TOE TAGZ I II

By Ah'Million

KINGPIN DREAMS

By Paper Boi Rari

CONFESSIONS OF A GANGSTA

By Nicholas Lock

I'M NOTHING WITHOUT HIS LOVE

By Monet Dragun

CAUGHT UP IN THE LIFE

By Robert Baptiste

NEW TO THE GAME

By **Malik D. Rice**

Life of a Savage

By **Romell Tukes**

LOYALTY AIN'T PROMISED

By Keith Williams

Quiet Money

By **Trai'Quan**

BOOKS BY LDP'S CEO, CA$H

TRUST IN NO MAN

TRUST IN NO MAN 2

TRUST IN NO MAN 3

BONDED BY BLOOD

SHORTY GOT A THUG

THUGS CRY

THUGS CRY 2

THUGS CRY 3

TRUST NO BITCH

TRUST NO BITCH 2

TRUST NO BITCH 3

TIL MY CASKET DROPS

RESTRAINING ORDER

RESTRAINING ORDER 2

IN LOVE WITH A CONVICT

Coming Soon

BONDED BY BLOOD 2

BOW DOWN TO MY GANGSTA

www.ingramcontent.com/pod-product-compliance
Lightning Source LLC
Chambersburg PA
CBHW070523260626
47161CB00004B/1626